THE CASE OF THE SHORTCAKE SERENADE

A Gossip Cozy Mystery Book 5

ROSIE A. POINT

The Case of the Shortcake Serenade
A Gossip Cozy Mystery Book 5

Join my no-spam newsletter and receive an exclusive offer. Details can be found at the back of this book.

Cover by Mariah Sinclair | TheCoverVault.com

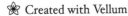 Created with Vellum

YOU'RE INVITED!

Hi there, reader!

I'd like to formally invite you to join my awesome community of readers. We love to chat about cozy mysteries, cooking, and pets.

It's super fun because I get to share chapters from yet-to-be-released books, fun recipes, pictures, and do giveaways with the people who enjoy my stories the most.

So whether you're a new reader or you've been enjoying my stories for a while, you can catch up with other like-minded readers, and get lots of cool content by visiting my website at *www.rosiepointbooks.com* and signing up for my mailing list.

Or simply search for me on *www.bookbub.com* and follow me there.

I look forward to getting to know you better.

Let's get into the story!

Yours,
Rosie

MEET THE CHARACTERS

Charlie Smith (Mission)—An ex-spy, Charlie's lives and works in her grandmother's inn in Gossip, Texas, as a server, maid, and assistant. With her particular set of skills and spunky attitude, she's become Gossip's "fixer" thanks to her previous involvement in solving murder mysteries.

Georgina Franklin (Mission)—Charlie's super-spy grandmother who raised her. Georgina (or Gamma, as Charlie calls her) is the most decorated spy in the history of the NSIB. She's retired, but still as smart and spry as ever.

Lauren Harris—The happy-go-lucky chef at the Gossip Inn. A master baker, she's always got delicious cupcakes prepared for the inn's lunches and dinners. She's jolly, with bright red hair she wears in pigtails.

Cocoa Puff—Georgina's chocolate brown cat. He's friendly as can be with people he trusts. Often sleeps on Charlie's bed and accompanies her around the inn, helping her dust the various trinkets and tables.

Sunlight—Charlie's newly adopted cat and co-sleuth. A ginger kitty with an adventurous spirit. He loves to get up to mischief in the inn and always has Charlie's back.

Jessie Belle-Blue—Jessie is Georgina's worst nightmare. As the owner of the local cattery and now, a guesthouse, she hates the fact that Georgina has opened a kitten foster center in direct competition. Will do whatever it takes to come out on top.

Detective Aaron Goode—The new tough detective in town. He's handsome, with dark hair, a strong jawline, and unflinching determination to get to the bottom of things. He doesn't appreciate interference.

"It's highly suspicious, and I've got to say, Charlie, I'm worried about it." Lauren, the Gossip Inn's happy-go-lucky chef, stood in front of the stove in the kitchen, a frown creasing her brow. "She's never done anything like this before."

All morning, Lauren had been stirring her pot of gravy and gossiping shamelessly about my grandmother, the owner of the inn, Georgina. Or Gamma as I liked to call her. Now, Lauren was as proficient at gossiping as everybody else in Gossip, Texas, but she'd never extended that behavior toward Gamma.

That meant something was seriously amiss.

Lauren gave another stir of her pot, her red eyebrows creeping upward. "She's been leaving the inn at strange hours of the morning. Usually, she stops by for a bite to eat and a cup of coffee when I arrive, but this morning?

Nothing. She didn't even greet me! It ain't right. Now, Charlie, you know I wouldn't talk ill of Georgina, I'd rather eat a jar of pickled peppers, but this is just too weird to ignore." Lauren brandished her spoon. "What if she's in trouble with... sinister forces?"

In Gamma's case, sinister forces could mean anything from her arch-enemy, Jessie Belle-Blue, a pashmina aficionado in need of a serious attitude adjustment, to an ex-arms dealer from Kuwait. That came with the territory when you were a retired ex-spy.

"I'm sure there's a perfectly rational explanation for Georgina's behavior," I said.

Of course, at the Gossip Inn, rational explanations usually involved spy work, fake ghosts, phantom cats, murderers and corpses, so that probably wasn't a comforting thing to say.

Lauren shivered delicately. "I still don't like it. This is not the right way to approach the holiday season."

"Laur, don't stress, OK? I'll talk to her about it," I said. "Besides, Georgina's a grown woman. She can look after herself." She could look after herself better than most Navy Seals.

Lauren muttered under her breath but returned to her pot stirring in silence.

It was just before the lunch service at the Gossip Inn, and there weren't too many guests at the moment. Most folks were at home with their families, and those who were staying here had been surprisingly docile. Which meant they weren't throwing tantrums or stealing the inn's cutlery. A fun positive for year-end.

But I was still caught up in my usual duties. Herding cats, catering to strange requests, and occasionally fixing a problem for one of the townsfolk.

Now that I thought about it, I'd been doing a lot more "fixing" than I had been cleaning the inn. Could it be that Gamma was upset with me about my lack of attentiveness to my usual duties? Just last week, I'd been asked to find a stolen jewelry box by a wealthier town resident, and I'd done it too. Granted, I'd found the jewelry box buried in the backyard—her Labrador had gotten into a habit of burying everything he could get his paws on—but it had kept me busy.

Busier than I'd thought possible in Gossip.

I glanced toward the kitchen doorway where the cats dozed in a line. Three of them, Snowy, the newest addition to the inn, was white as her name, Cocoa Puff, brown, sweet, and lazy, and Sunlight, who was a ginger kitty and full of mischief.

Sunlight was my cat, whereas Cocoa and Snowy belonged to the inn, but I loved them equally. Dearly.

I gnawed on my bottom lip.

What if it's... time?

"Charlie?" Lauren's voice brought me back from my musings.

I turned to her. "Right. Sorry. What do you need me to do?" I'd also been neglecting my duties as Lauren's helper in the kitchen. It was a quieter time, so she'd been managing everything by herself, but I still felt guilt over it.

"Nothing in particular," Lauren said. "I'm just curious about what's on your mind."

I went over to the cats and gave each of them a scratch behind the ears, considering my answer.

Lauren waited patiently, using the time to lay out dishes on the countertops.

"I'm thinking about my future," I said, truthfully. "At the inn, mainly." By this point, I'd figured out that I did fit into Gossip. I might not have been used to small town living when I'd first arrived, but I'd grown to love it. In a big city, there was anonymity, but there was a lot less "care" than there was in Gossip, at least in my experience.

"What about it?" Lauren asked, watching me as she worked. "I know you've been a little busier than usual of late."

"A lot busier," I said. "I know I haven't exactly been helping that much."

"Now, don't say that. You've got your own stuff going on. I'm sure that being an assistant at the Gossip Inn was never your long term plan."

That was true, of course. I had arrived at the inn over

a year ago, only because it was the best place for me to hide out from my rogue spy ex-husband, Kyle Turner. Now, that was over. He was behind bars for good, and I was retired. Free to live my life how I pleased, as long as I didn't draw too much attention to myself.

Working at the inn had been a cover, never a life choice.

But I loved it here.

"Charlie?"

"I don't know," I said, at last. "I love the inn. I love the kitten foster center. I love being around the cats, though I could do without all the guests, particularly the grumpy ones." I paused, considering. "I think what I'd like is to start my own business. Be the problem fixer for Gossip. Maybe have my own place to live?"

"And leave the inn?" Lauren sounded scandalized, hurt even.

That was what I'd been afraid of. And if Lauren reacted like that, I could only imagine how my grandmother would feel.

"Nothing's decided yet," I said, smiling at her. "Come on, let's focus on the lunch service."

Lauren wriggled her nose. "Aw, Charlie, I didn't mean to discourage you. I guess, I just can't imagine the inn without you anymore. You're as much a part of the Gossip Inn as the cats or Georgina herself."

"Or you," I said.

She colored a pleasant pink. "You're too sweet. And you're right. Let's finish setting up the—"

A shrill scream rang out from the hallway. All three cats leaped to their feet and scattered in different directions.

"Help me! Please," the cry came. A woman yelling at the top of her lungs. "Charlotte Smith. I need your help!"

I turned around and darted from the kitchen, my pulse racing.

2

A crowd had gathered on the first floor landing of the stairs, looking down into the Gossip Inn's foyer, with its chandelier and nooks containing tables bearing trinkets. The guests clasped their throats, covered their mouths or looked on in horror at the spectacle unfolding before their eyes.

If it could be called that. Folks in Gossip had a penchant for blowing things way out of proportion. I wasn't sure if every small town was the same, but drama hung over the town in a nearly perceptible mist.

A woman knelt in the middle of the foyer, right on the gorgeous Persian carpet, clutching her skirt in two fistfuls. Her dark hair fell around her shoulders in glossy waves, and her young, beautiful face was stricken with grief. She sobbed theatrically then threw herself forward, stretching her arms out in desperation, reaching for me.

Honestly, it reminded me of a scene out of a telenovela, and I was both alarmed and entertained.

"Ma'am?" I came forward and stopped just short of her scrabbling fingers. "Ma'am, are you OK? Do you need medical assistance?"

She choked out three hiccuping sobs. "I-I-I-I need your h-h-help."

"With what?" I asked.

A quick assessment told me that she wasn't injured. And she could talk and seemed lucid. I wanted to rule out a head injury, but then she *had* just flung herself onto the floor at my feet.

"Please." She pushed herself upright then shifted hair from her face, looking up at me through teary eyes. "Please, you must help me. I can't... I need... Please!" Another dramatic sob and bout of writhing on the floor.

Knowing that I hadn't vacuumed all week made this worse. A cold wind, thankfully, it was never too bitterly cold in Texas, drifted through the inn's front doors.

I straightened my apron, sighed, then extended a hand to the woman. "Come on," I said. "You're clearly in shock. You need some sugar." I helped her up, and she clung to me, still weeping. "Sorry about this, everyone." I called that to the guests. "I'm just going to make sure this woman is all right, but lunch will be served on time today, as usual."

No one replied.

At least they'd get lunch and they'd had a show, right?

I wish Gamma was here. Gamma would've taken control of the situation instantly, perhaps even sent everyone off to their rooms before incapacitating the emotional woman with a pinch to the correct nerve cluster in the neck.

I guided the weeping woman into the kitchen and fed her into a chair at the square table. She bonked her head down on the table and continued to cry.

"Goodness, Charlie," Lauren said, "you know the rules by now. No guests in the kitchen. It's illegal." Not technically true, but then again, Gossip had a lot of strange laws.

"It was this or I threw a bucket of water over her, and I didn't want to ruin the carpet." Gamma was particularly attached to her new carpet. She'd found it online at what she claimed was a "steal." Knowing her, she'd really gotten it from one of her illegal contacts. They dealt in everything from RPGs to state of the art truth serums to ancient artefacts.

"I suppose," Lauren grumbled. "Fix her some hot chocolate. I'll take the food out to the dining room."

"Are you sure?" I asked. "I mean, you might need—"

"Don't worry about it." Lauren gave me a sweet smile, and I returned it. Lauren was often willing to take on loads that she shouldn't, and it was my fault, once again, that she was in this position.

The fact that the weeping woman had called out my name had to mean she was here because she'd heard I was a "fixer."

I prepared a mug of hot chocolate for her then brought it back and set it on the kitchen table. "There you go," I said. "Drink up." I wasn't the best with emotional conversations, but I had learned a few things from Lauren and Gamma. "It will help you feel better."

The woman lifted her head from the table, slowly, and gave me a bleary-eyed stare. Her bottom lip trembled. "T-t-thank you," she whispered.

I wanted to feel sorry for her, but I'd had a similar encounter with a woman a couple of weeks ago and it had been because she'd lost her designer handbag. Needless to say, I would retain my cynicism until I had a reason not to.

The woman lifted her mug and took a sip. A chocolate mustache remained on her top lip.

"What's your name?" I asked.

"M-M-Mia Cruz," she said.

"Right. Mia. Nice to meet you. What can I help you with?" I sat down in the chair opposite hers and rested my elbows on the table.

I was sure this would either be an interesting case or about something completely mundane.

"My boyfriend, Donny, has been murdered."

An interesting case!

"And the police think I'm the one who did it!" Mia finished, releasing it as a wail. Though, I couldn't help noticing that her stammer was gone. "You have to help me. I can't stand the thought of them accusing me of this when I've done nothing wrong, and I've lost my dearest Donny. My love. The man who was going to be my husband."

She couldn't have been a day over twenty-one. That seemed young to be married, but, then again, I was a commitment-phobe at this point.

"OK," I said. "Let's start from the beginning." This wasn't my first time talking to a family member or loved one who was involved in a murder case. We had to progress through this step-by-step. If Mia wound up being the one who had done it, it wouldn't be the first time I had been approached by the victim of a crime who was actually the perpetrator. People were weird like that.

"The beginning," Mia said.

"Yes. Tell me what happened."

"It's all so confusing. I don't even understand *how* it happened. One second he was serenading me, the next he was..." She made a choked noise in her throat.

"Wait, he was serenading you?"

"Yes," she said, and her eyelashes fluttered. "My

Donny loved to serenade me. He adored me, you see, treated me like I was his princess."

"What's Donny's full name?" I asked.

"Donny Braxton."

"OK. And now, when was the last time you saw him, and what happened to him?"

Mia took a deep, shuddering breath. "So, he, well, I—"

"It's OK. Take your time." *It's not like your boyfriend's corpse is cooling somewhere or anything.* Man, I really did have too much of a cynical side sometimes. It was the ex-spy, the Charlotte Mission part of me, rearing her head.

Mia fortified herself with another sip of hot chocolate. "Donny came over to my house last night," she said. "I-I didn't let him in because we were in the middle of a fight."

"A fight? Over what?"

"I don't really see how that's important, right now," Mia half-sobbed.

"You never know what might be important in a case like this," I said, leaning back in my chair. "I need to know everything I can before I even decide to help fix your problem."

That got her attention. She straightened in her chair and placed her Christmas mug off to one side. "Right, OK. Right. Donny and I had been arguing because I was tired of waiting for him to propose. I told him that either he had to give me a ring or it was over. He came by last night to try to win me over again."

"OK, so he came by and then what happened?"

"He started singing underneath my window," Mia said. "One of my favorite songs. 'Drop It Like It's Hot' by Snoop Dogg."

I swallowed a snort. That wasn't exactly the most, uh, appropriate song around. "Did you invite him in?"

"No," she said. "My mother hates Donny. Thinks he's a player or whatever, which is a total lie, but that's beside the point. I was still mad at him, so I threw a shoe at him, and then I shut my windows and went to bed. He stopped singing about a half an hour later. And then—oh, it's just, it's terrible. My mom woke up this morning and found him on the front lawn. Dead!" That came out in another emotional screech. "And now the cops think that I did it. Because of my shoe. I just... I need your help, please. Help me figure out what really happened to Donny. My mother will pay you to help me."

Why would your mother pay me when she couldn't stand your boyfriend? That alone intrigued me.

I had gotten to the point where I could deny new cases if I wanted, even murder cases, especially if it meant I would step on Detective Goode's toes.

My heart did a gymnastic flip at the thought of the handsome detective who had kissed me on Thanksgiving Day.

I swallowed, shoving that thought aside.

"Please. Help me."

I stared at Mia for a few seconds, taking in the expression of wide-eyed innocence that I was fairly certain was fake. "OK," I said. "I'll take the case."

❦ 3 ❦

After the lunch service was done, and I had received the first portion of my fee from Mia Cruz's mother, I borrowed my grandmother's Mini-Cooper and set off. I was excited for a new case, but nervous as well, and a little worried about Gamma. She was missing in action, lately, and while I wasn't the type of person who pried into people's business—maybe that was why I'd failed as a spy—I still worried, no matter how much I told Lauren not to.

The Cruz family home was a double-story, located in one of the middle-class neighborhoods of Gossip. It had a big front yard, a flat, concrete pathway that led up to a simple porch with a merry green front door.

The upstairs window on the right, a sash window, was open despite the chill in the air, the curtains in it hanging limply.

I parked the Mini-Cooper on the verge and got out of the car, sweeping fingers through my short blonde hair, and studying the scene.

The house looked... well, frankly, like it would be easy to break into. The upstairs window was open, the front door ajar, and no fences or gates guarding the property. The road was also wide and open, and the houses on either side had plenty of trees and bushes for a potential attacker to hide in.

"Miss Smith?" A woman appeared on the porch. She was slim and gorgeous, with her dark hair in a bun atop her head. "Hello."

"Mrs. Cruz?" This had to be Mia's mother. They looked awfully similar.

"That's me." She came down the stairs and shook my hand. "Thank you so much for coming out today. This has been a tragedy for Mia. And it's only getting worse. I can't believe that idiot Detective's nerve to come out here and..." She trailed off, shaking her head. "Anyway, that doesn't matter right now. We've got you to help us."

I forced a smile.

Whenever anyone referred to Detective Goode, my stomach would erupt into butterflies. I couldn't help thinking about him romantically, even though he had the ability to make me mad beyond belief.

"I'm happy to help," I said. "But I'll need more details than I've already received."

"Right, of course. One second." She retreated back toward the house, poked her head around the front door and yelled. "Mia! Mia, the fixer is here to see us. Hurry up!"

A crash came from inside, and Mia rattled out of the house a few seconds later. Both women joined me. They stood next to each other, but with a fair amount of space between them. Interesting.

My grandmother would've told me to read into the behavioral cues that people gave out without even realizing it, and so, I made a mental note of the gap between them. Did they not get along?

Mia had told me that her mother didn't approve of her relationship with Donny. Could that be the problem?

I brought my small pad and stubby pencil, a habit I'd formed when investigating cases like this, and smiled at the women. "OK, so I have a few questions."

"Fire away," Mrs. Cruz said.

Mia cast a sidelong glance at her mother.

"First, where did you find Mr. Braxton's body?" I asked.

"Right there." Mrs. Cruz pointed to a patch of grass that was directly beneath the open window on the second floor. "He was sort of half in and out of the flowerbed."

Mia covered her mouth and took deep, huffing breaths.

"About what time was this?" I asked.

"It must have been 06:00 a.m. because that's when I leave for work," Mrs. Cruz said.

I paused, making a note of that. "And you last saw him at what time, Mia?"

"10:00 p.m., just before I went to bed," Mia squeaked.

Another quick note. I hesitated. How to word this delicately? The last thing I wanted was for Mia to throw herself onto the ground again and roll around, wailing. "You didn't see the body, did you Mia?"

She shook her head.

"Then, Mrs. Cruz, would you be so kind as to tell me exactly what you saw? In as much detail as possible. Sorry." I grimaced.

"That's fine," Mrs. Cruz said, apparently unfazed by the whole event. "I'll do what I can to help clear Mia's name."

But not to help figure out who committed the crime? Mrs. Cruz hadn't liked Donny Braxton one bit, was my wager. I'd have to find out more about him. Could there be a specific reason she hadn't liked him?

"I came out just before work, and I saw him just lying there in the yard. At first I thought he had passed out after making all that noise the night before, but yeah, he was dead. Knife in the back."

"I can't handle this!" Mia screamed, then turned on her heel and fled back into the house.

Mrs. Cruz rolled her eyes so hard, her eyelashes fluttered. "You'll have to forgive my daughter. She's dramatic even when her friend hasn't been murdered."

"Friend? I thought he was Mia's boyfriend?"

Mrs. Cruz pursed her lips. "I doubt he could commit to being her boyfriend. Mr. Braxton was... not the type of man who settled down. Let me put it that way. And he certainly wasn't good enough for my Mia."

Upstairs the sash window slammed shut, and a furious and pale Mia stared down at us from above.

"You have no idea what it's like dealing with a daughter who won't see sense. She wouldn't listen to me about him. She didn't care about the rumors in town. That he was a player. That he was dating multiple young women her age. There was nothing I could do, and now he's dead, and I'm stuck worrying about Mia's future. That low-life didn't even have the decency to—" She stopped talking, abruptly, as if realizing she'd said a little too much.

OK. So she hated the guy. "Tell me more about the crime scene, please." My stubby pencil hovered over the page of my notebook. The more details I got, the better. I'd be able to take them back to Gamma and discuss them with her at length.

My grandmother was always looking for a side project

—it was difficult to feel fulfilled after living the life of a spy—and she often took part in my cases.

My cases. It was strange to think of them that way, but I had reached that point now. I spent more time thinking about mysteries than I did dusting. And dusting happened to be my favorite thing to do at the Gossip Inn.

"The crime scene," Mrs. Cruz said, and pulled a face. "There was blood, and he was stabbed, but I didn't see a knife or anything. Oh, and there was a box of shortcake next to the body."

"That's a lie!" The sash window above had been opened again. Mia clasped the sill and leaned out, glaring down at us. "There's no way he brought me shortcake."

"What's wrong with shortcake?" I asked.

"Nothing. Shortcake is delicious," Mrs. Cruz said. "Usually. I mean the box was... well, you wouldn't want to eat shortcake that had been sitting next to a corpse."

"You're disgusting, mother," Mia cried. "Disgusting."

"Why wouldn't Donny have brought you shortcake, Mia?" I called up to her.

She chewed on her bottom lip. "Because I hate shortcake. It's gross. He wouldn't have come all the way out here to sing to me and apologize with a box of shortcake."

"Maybe the shortcake wasn't for you, honey," her mother said, pointedly.

The window slapped shut again.

"OK," I said. "OK, where were we?" I noted down the lack of murder weapon, the shortcake, and the cause of death.

"I don't know," Mrs. Cruz said. "Things have been so complicated lately. The detective keeps coming by to talk to us. You see, they found one of Mia's shoes in the flowerbed and they think she's involved because of it. If only they knew how pathetically obsessed she was with the man. She would never have killed him."

People had murdered in the name of "love." Obsession was easy to mistake for it. "She mentioned she threw a shoe down at him because she was mad about an argument they had."

"Right." But the shifty-eyed glance up at the window told me she hadn't known that particular detail.

What was going on here between mother and daughter. Could the mother have wanted to get rid of Donny so badly she'd killed him?

"Did you hear anything last night?" I wagered that Donny had to have been stabbed shortly after Mia had shut her window. The fact that he had been found below her window had to mean he hadn't gotten the chance to walk off.

The trouble was, the street was completely open as was the yard. It would've been easy for a potential attacker to sneak up on the victim, stab him, and then run off never to be seen again.

"No, not really. I don't think so. I heard Donny singing. I heard my daughter's window slam, and then there was a strange bang and silence. I don't know what the bang was. It sounded like something hitting the wall. Maybe it was Donny falling over?"

She's so calm about this. "And where were you last night?"

"Here," she said, stiffly. "At the house."

"And your daughter?"

"She was here too. She went to bed after she closed her window. That's what she told me," Mrs. Cruz said.

"You didn't say goodnight to her?"

"I was busy."

Smell that? Steaming, hot lies. I couldn't wait to talk to Gamma. This case was complicated. Without having seen the crime scene or the body, I was short on clues or leads.

"And do you know of anyone who might have wanted to hurt Donny?" I asked.

Mrs. Cruz licked her lips, a little flick of the tongue over them, like a snake. "I don't know. I guess any one of his many girlfriends or their parents."

I made a note of it. I'd have to find out more about that. I studied what I'd written down so far. "Two more questions, Mrs. Cruz, if you'll bear with me?"

"Sure. Go ahead. Whatever I can do to help," she said.

"First, do you know if any of your neighbors have a door cam? Do you?"

"No, sorry. We don't have cameras in this street. It's a privacy issue."

Because privacy is more of a concern than security. "And then, lastly, do you know where the shortbread came from? You said it was in a box. Did it come from a specific bakery in town, maybe?" This year, I'd spent a lot of time working on a case that revolved around the many bakeries in Gossip. One of them was run by Lauren's sister, who happened to be a real pain in the neck.

Please don't say the Little Cake Shop. Please don't say the Little Cake Shop.

"Yeah, it was from the Little Cake Shop."

Just my luck. I shoved my pad and pencil into my pocket again. "Thank you for your time, Mrs. Cruz. I'll let you know how things go."

4

I frowned and checked my phone for the third time in as many minutes. I sat on a bench under an oak tree in the inn's front yard, waiting for Gamma to make her presence known. This was our rendezvous point, come rain or shine, and I'd texted her to meet me here forty-five minutes ago. It was unlike her to be late, especially when there was an interesting development to dissect.

Life in Gossip was slow, and Gamma liked to keep an eye on everyone and everything that happened in town. So where was she?

Footsteps crunched on the gravel pathway, and my grandmother appeared, a spring in her step and a smile gracing her features.

"Charlotte," she said.

"It's been forty-five minutes," I replied. "Are you OK?"

"Goodness, since when are you a time lord?" Gamma's prim British accent was always more pronounced when she was irritable. Or happy. Any type of emotion, really. "I didn't mean to keep you waiting. I was just... preoccupied."

"With?"

"Nothing of consequence." Gamma lowered herself onto the bench beside me, tucking her skirt underneath herself. "Now, tell me what you've discovered. I hear we've lost another valuable member of the Gossip community."

"Was that sarcasm?"

Gamma shook her head. "Oh no. I don't joke about death. Unless it's the death of someone truly evil, and I know that Mr. Braxton was not truly evil. Though, no one called him Mr. Braxton. He was Donny to everyone."

Briefly, I told my grandmother what had happened this morning at the inn—the over the top reaction from Mia and then the interesting encounter I'd had with her mother. "I think there's something going on there. Do you know anything about them? Or the victim?"

"Oh, I know plenty, but I can do a little extra research regarding all the major suspects and the victim. I'll put my feelers out. Ask the grapes."

Gamma had a "grapevine" of informants who told her

all about the goings on in Gossip. It was likely how she'd known about Donny's death before I'd messaged her.

"Mia and her mother do not get along," Gamma said. "And Mia is an aspiring model. Wants to leave Gossip behind and head out to the big city, last I heard, but her mother forbade it."

"That's interesting."

"How so?"

"Mia mentioned that she'd fought with Donny this week because he hadn't proposed to her. Why would she want him to propose if she planned on leaving Gossip? Weird."

Gamma fell silent, mulling it over and tapping her fingers on her knees. She definitely seemed more upbeat than usual. "Now, that is interesting. I'll have to talk to some people before I give you feedback on that."

"What about Donny?" I asked. "Mia's mother had some pretty choice things to say about him."

"I don't blame her," Gamma said. "I've always detested a man who thinks it prudent to date multiple women at the same time. Somehow, it's frowned upon for women to do that but with men, it's to be expected. Ridiculous. I'm of the school of thought that all men and women should behave respectfully."

"Thanks for the lecture, Georgina."

She grinned at me, good naturedly. "Donny was a mechanic. Handsome as they came, and he loved to play the field. He made a lot of enemies because of that, whether they were ex-boyfriends of the ladies he dated or the parents. Murder, though? It seems a bit much."

"A bit," I agreed. "But Mrs. Cruz definitely fits the bill when it comes to disgruntled parents. She might have motive. And if Mia's lying about her argument with—"

Footsteps came on the gravel driveway a second time, and I cut off. Both Gamma and I turned in our seats.

Detective Goode strode toward us, his hands tucked into the pockets of his jeans so that he swaggered rather than walked.

My heart did another silly somersault. *Ugh. Get over it, Charlie.*

"Good afternoon, ladies."

"Detective Goode," Gamma said. "I'm going to assume you haven't come to speak to me."

"Unless you've robbed any banks lately."

"The Gossip Bank was robbed?" Gamma asked, incredulous.

"No," he said, and cleared his throat. "That was a joke." Detective Goode was dark-haired and handsome, with a strong jawline and eyes that cut right through me.

"Ah, well," Gamma replied, "yet more proof that comedy isn't for everyone."

I snorted a laugh.

Gamma grinned at me. "I'll leave you two alone." She rose and walked off a distance before glancing back at

Detective Goode. "I hope you're not another Don Juan, Detective Goode. Apparently, they don't live long around these parts." That was a reference to the romantic mechanic, Donny, who had just died. And it was definitely a threat from my grandmother.

Detective Goode had the good grace to gulp. Although, it might've been his true reaction to the threat. Gamma had a knack for scaring men and women alike with her intense stares.

She left us together, disappearing into the inn.

An awkward silence sidled into place.

Detective Goode cleared his throat. "So."

"So?" I stared up at him, refusing to look flustered even though I felt like fifty million ants were crawling over my skin.

"How are you?" he asked, scuffing the underside of his boot across the gravel. He kept distance between us.

"I'm great. How are you?"

"Great. Good. Fine."

Wait, was *he* flustered too? So far, Detective Goode had been nothing but in charge and remarkably annoying.

"OK. Well, glad you came all the way down here and interrupted my conversation with Georgina to tell me that," I said.

Goode flashed me an irritable smile. "I came here because we haven't talked since Thanksgiving."

Thanksgiving. The day he had kissed me. The day I had blushed too many shades of red and pink to count. Over the past couple of weeks, I'd been focusing on being a fixer, on trying to figure out what I wanted to do after the Christmas season. And actively avoiding thoughts about the handsome detective. He hadn't called or come by. I'd assumed that he hadn't wanted a kiss or a date anymore.

"Right," I said. "You want to talk, so talk."

"Sheesh. Tough crowd."

"The last time you were here, you kissed me and then you left," I said, putting it plain as day. "And then you didn't talk to me for weeks. So, you expect me to be polite? My life is complicated enough already without men thrown into the mix."

Goode opened his mouth then shut it again.

I stared him down, waiting.

After a minute, I rose and made to leave.

"Wait," he choked it out. "I'm not good with... this kind of stuff."

Me neither.

"I want to take you out on a date," he said. "For real this time."

"A date," I replied. "And you promise not to arrest me during the appetizers?" *You aren't seriously going to say yes, are you?*

Goode gave me a cocky grin. "Don't break the law again and I won't have to."

"It was never proven that I broke the law," I countered. "The charges were dropped."

Goode kept on grinning, and so did I. So we stood, like two loons, smiling goofily at one another.

"Would you like to go out with me on Friday?" he asked. "At eight?"

I considered. A part of me wanted to close off the thought, and another...? Well, I wanted to live in Gossip, didn't I? And what harm was there in going out with a handsome law enforcement official? Particularly one who might give me details about the Donny Braxton case?

"Fine," I said. "But don't be late." I spun on my heel and marched off, hoping I looked more serious than I felt.

5

Josie Carlson was the opposite to her sister, Lauren, in nearly every way. She had darker hair, was large, full of bluster, and liked conflict. Lauren always had a kind word to say about people in town, even if it was in the middle of a juicy gossip session, but Josie... she'd rather eat her own apron than say something *nice*.

The Little Cake Shop was on a street with several bakeries and patisseries, and those delicious smells wafted in the air, tempting passersby to stop and grab a bite to eat or a cup of coffee.

Funny how the smell of baking bread and cupcakes gave me anxiety instead. But, eh, that was just when I was in this street. Back at the Gossip Inn, I couldn't get enough baked goods thanks to Lauren's culinary stylings.

I passed a few familiar faces as I approached the bakery and smiled or greeted them. I was used to the warmth of the people in Gossip by now, but it still struck me as different every now and again.

I entered the Little Cake Shop, with its inviting glass front doors, cream and blue awning, and floor to ceiling windows, and joined the line arcing toward the counters at the back of the room.

The smell of cupcakes intensified accompanied by fresh-brewed coffee.

I spotted Josie exiting the office behind the counter and flagged her down like she was a particularly grumpy trucker and I was a hitchhiker.

"What do you want?" Josie asked, raising an eyebrow at me.

Yeah, we weren't on the best of terms. I'd been honest with Lauren about how I felt about Josie, and the last time I'd encountered her, well, that hadn't exactly gone well either.

"Good morning," I said, as pleasantly as I could muster. "How are you today?"

Josie gave me a blank stare in return.

So much for the advancements I'd made in my people skills, right? "Mind if I talk to you for a second? Alone? It's important."

"Come to accuse me of murder again?" Josie asked.

"Thankfully, no," I replied, bringing up a smile. "But I think you might be able to help me with a case."

"And *why* would I want to help *you?*"

"Lauren would want you to," I said, simply.

Lauren and Josie had an *interesting* relationship. I'd always figured Josie was the bossy, in charge sister until I'd seen her mess up and watched as Lauren took charge.

Josie wriggled her nose from side-to-side then sighed, at last. "Fine," she said. "Fine. Come with me."

I followed her around the counter and into her cramped office. She sat down behind her desk, watching me, warily.

"Thanks for your help," I said.

"I haven't helped you yet."

"Right," I replied. "But I'm sure you'll be able to. I wanted to talk to you about Donny Braxton. Do you know him?"

"Sure. Donny comes by the bakery every week," she said. "He picks up his regular order and leaves right afterward. Piece of trash."

I blinked. "Trash?"

"Yeah," Josie said, and studied her stubby nails. "He's trash. Man trash, if you get what I mean."

"Why's that?"

"Because he likes to date around. He thinks he's a regular Don Juan. You know, always romancing women and then leaving them in the lurch when they need them most..."

"Did *you* date him Josie?"

"Me?" She colored, the tiniest tinge of pink in her

cheeks. "When we were in high school, years ago. When he was still relatively OK. Now he's trouble."

"But you didn't have a problem with him."

"No, not really. I didn't really talk to him. I'd see him sometimes when he came in, but other than that, we didn't talk or know each other that well anymore. People change."

I nodded.

"Why are you asking questions about him, for heaven's sake? Let me guess, one of his girlfriends has hired you to tail him and find out what he's been up to?" Josie's eyes lit up at the prospect. Gossip was practically a currency in this town.

"Not quite," I said. "Donny's dead. I've been asked to find out what happened to him." Technically, I'd been asked to clear a suspects name, but my ethical code—the same rather shaky code that allowed me to kidnap and question suspects when necessary—dictated that I find the killer instead. Even if that killer turned out to be my client.

"Dead." Josie sat back in her chair, pinching the edge of her desk with her fingertips. "He's dead? Really?"

"Really. I thought you would've heard. It's big news. He was stabbed."

"Stabbed. Wow. Poor Donny," she said. "I mean, I can't say I didn't see this coming. He caused trouble wherever he went."

"Man trash?" I repeated her phrase from earlier.

She glared at me. "I wasn't being disrespectful of the dead. I didn't know."

"I'm not accusing you of anything, Josie. I'm just interested in a few things, particularly when it comes to Donny's behavior. You said he came by to pick up a regular order."

"Yeah."

"What did he buy from you?"

"Shortcake," she said. "Every week on a Monday, he comes by to pick up an order of shortcake."

"Do you know who it was for?" I asked.

"I assumed it was for him, but I don't know. No. Sorry."

So, Donny had been buying a box of shortcake for *somebody*—maybe himself—for weeks now. "Two days ago, when he came to pick up the box of shortcake, did you notice anything strange about his behavior?"

"No, not really. I barely registered he was here. I just gave him his order as usual." Josie wrinkled her brow and squidged her eyes closed for a second. "Wait. Wait, I do remember something. He went out onto the side-walk, and he kind of looked behind himself as he walked off. Like he was expecting someone to be there?"

"Which direction did he go in?"

Josie turned her head as she oriented herself. "Toward

the Hungry Steer," she said. "So left once you hit the sidewalk."

"Great. Thank you."

Josie rolled her eyes like she'd rather have done anything other than help me. Which was probably not far from the truth. I headed for the office door then paused and looked back. "One last thing."

"Sure. I have... so much time to talk to you. It's not like I'm a busy business woman or anything."

"Do you know of anyone who might've wanted to hurt Donny? Names, specifically."

"I don't know who he was dating and I don't care," Josie said, "but he had a brother. Noah. Noah Braxton. He's a writer." Josie snorted like that was the most ridiculous occupation on the planet. "Lives off his mother's money."

"Do you know where he lives?"

"Sure, everybody does. On Old Park Street. Number 534. He's got one of those ridiculous flamingos in his front yard. You can't miss it," Josie said.

I thanked her one last time, receiving nothing but a disdainful stare in return, then slipped out into the bakery.

I had a thread to tug on, and I couldn't wait to pull on it and unravel the case.

6

I liked the pink flamingo in the front yard. It gave the house, a squat brick box, some personality that was much needed. I emerged from Gamma's sea-green Mini-Cooper and dusted off my jeans, studying Noah Braxton's house and the others in the street.

It was a quiet area. Not particularly well-to-do, lower middle class at best, but safe. Most of Gossip was safe, apart from when there was a murderer on the loose, of course.

A door slammed somewhere nearby, and a car started. A silver sedan cruised by, the woman behind the wheel raising her fingers as she drove by. I had no clue who she was, but this was Gossip. Everybody greeted in Gossip.

I waved back before setting off up the front path and past the pink flamingo that had been stuck in the long grass beside it.

A quick knock on the front door later, and a tall, handsome man met me, smiling broadly. He had perfectly even white teeth, so even, in fact, that it was kind of unsettling.

"Hello," I said, presenting a hand. "My name is Charlotte Smith." I still had to stop myself from saying "Mission" instead of "Smith." Another reason I hadn't been a particularly good spy.

"Noah Braxton." He shook my hand, delicately. His palm was clammy, and I resisted the urge to wipe my hands on my jeans, afterward.

"Nice to meet you," I said.

"Sure." He frowned, and the already pronounced wrinkles furrowed even more. "Is there a reason we're meeting?"

"Sorry," I laughed. "Yeah. I'm here because I've been trying to figure out who harmed your brother." Harmed was less visceral than the word "murdered."

Noah's face fell, his eyes grew watery, and he swallowed audibly. "Right," he said. "Donny. Our Donny."

"I'm so sorry for your loss."

He exhaled, releasing the breath in a long, low stream. "Thank you. It's been a difficult past few days."

"I can only imagine," I replied. "I was hired by a close friend of Donny's to find out who could've done this."

"Excuse me for asking," Noah said, "but why would they have hired you?"

THE CASE OF THE SHORTCAKE SERENADE

"I'm a fixer. Kind of like a private investigator." The difference was, private investigators usually didn't have experience as spies. "And I'm trying to get to the bottom of what happened. I had a couple of specific questions for you, if you have the time to answer them? I understand this is a difficult time..."

Noah sighed, glancing over his shoulder. He exited onto the porch and shut the door, favoring his left leg a little. He had a limp. That was interesting. Was there a story behind that?

Noah gestured for me to sit down on the front step with him.

It wasn't the most orthodox place I'd interviewed a suspect, but it also wasn't the weirdest. I sat down, pressing my back into the railing so I could study the side of Noah's face while he talked.

"I haven't talked to anyone about Donny except the police," Noah said.

"Do you feel comfortable talking to me?"

"I'm curious," Noah said. "Not comfortable. You see, I'm a novelist. A romance novelist most specifically, and I'm always looking to experience new things. A fixer? That's interesting to me. I'll answer your questions if you answer some of mine."

An information trade. This guy was decidedly strange, but I'd go with it if it meant getting answers.

"OK, sure," I said. "You go first."

"So, what does a fixer do, exactly?" he asked.

"I fix problems. It can be anything from a small problem to a big one, but I always operate within the confines of the law." Man, that was a lie. Just last month I'd been arrested for interfering in one of Goode's investigations.

"Interesting. And do you usually fix the problems successfully?"

"I have a one hundred percent success rate so far."

Noah smiled. "Cool. You can ask me your questions now."

"That's all you wanted to know?" I asked.

"Uh-huh, yeah."

This guy didn't give me the creeps or anything, but there was something off about him. Maybe it was just because he was one of those creative types. You never knew with them. Head always in the clouds, floating along with no real concept of the world happening around them. Of course, they were a necessary part of society, but I preferred practical people like Gamma or Lauren.

"I've been told that your brother bought a box of shortcake at The Little Cake Shop every Monday. Is that correct?" *Will Noah even know this information?*

"Yeah, actually," Noah said. "Donny lived with me, and he used to dip out every Monday to go grab that cake. It was how I found out about Emmy."

"Emmy?"

"Emmy Scott," Noah said. "Donny's fiancee."

I kept my expression impassive. *Goodness. Donny was a player, all right.* "He bought the cake for her every Monday?" I asked.

"Every Monday evening. He would grab the cake then head on over to see her."

OK, so he'd bought the cake to take to his fiancee, but he'd stopped at his girlfriend's house first. Where someone had murdered him.

"Did you see Donny on Monday?"

"Only before he left the house," Noah said. "I had a big deadline to meet for my book, so I was in all day."

"What about in the evening?"

"Unfortunately, no. You see, I was at a party with Emmy."

I rubbed my brow. "Wait, you were at a party with Emmy? Your brother's fiancee?"

"Yeah. We were all in the same friend group, you see. So we were hanging out on Monday night, waiting for Donny to come over. We were playing cards and watching TV, listening to music, that kind of thing."

"What time?" I asked. "As in, what time did you arrive at Emmy's house and when did you leave?"

Noah shrugged. "Oh, that's tricky. I think I got there at like six in the evening? Left at eleven, maybe. I really didn't make much note of the time. It was nice to get out, though, after a long day of writing. It's so easy to just lock myself away indoors for long periods of time. I have to force myself to be social."

I absorbed the information.

I had another suspect to add to my list. The fiancee, Emmy Scott. She could've easily found out about Mia, the girlfriend, and planned to get rid of Donny. But why not just leave him? Dump him? Surely, murdering him was too risky and kind of pointless?

And hadn't Josie told me about Noah, the brother, for a reason?

"Did you and Donny get on?" I asked. "Were you close? Ever get into fights or anything like that"

"Fights? Nothing beyond the normal sibling stuff. We were very close," Noah said, and those tears welled again, shimmering in his dark eyes. "We were... friends and brothers. Donny was a romantic, just like me, except he acted out his romantic aspirations whereas I prefer to write about them. Do you really think you can find out who did this?"

"Yes," I said. "I'm going to try my level best." And so far, my level best had proved very effective. But I needed to think about my leads and plan my next steps.

If what Noah had said was true, he had an alibi, as did Emmy, if he'd only left the friend get-together at 11:00 p.m.. Donny had been stabbed around 10:00 p.m..

"Do you need anything else from me?" Noah asked. "I don't mean to be rude but there's a lot to organize now that Donny's gone. We don't have... parents anymore. No close relatives. I'm all he had."

"That's all," I said. "Thank you for your help, Noah."

7

That afternoon...

I HAD TEXTED GAMMA TWICE IN THE LAST HOUR, AND she'd read both messages without replying. Again, most unlike her. Was Lauren right? Should I be worried about the strange behavior? Silly. Even if I was worried, there wasn't much I could do about it short of asking Gamma what was up.

The truth was, if my grandmother, the most decorated spy in NSIB history, wanted to hide her activity from us, she'd do it without too much effort.

I sat outside the hair salon in town, parked in the Mini-Cooper with the windows cracked to allow in the brisk breeze, waiting.

Apparently, Emmy Scott worked at the salon. I'd gotten a description of her from Lauren. Tall, pretty, with cherry red hair and freckles.

I'd already spotted her in there, chatting away with her clients, but I didn't have anywhere else to be, and I needed time to think about the case, so I was in no rush to head inside the salon. To be frank, salons stressed me out. The last time I'd been in one, I'd been forced to change my natural hair to something much more bushy and cumbersome.

Yet another reason I'd made a poor spy.

"OK," I muttered, and brought my notepad and pencil out of my purse. I leaned the notepad against the steering wheel and started my note-taking, glancing up now and again to make sure Emmy hadn't disappeared.

Victim

Donny Braxton. Local lothario who had quite a few enemies. Apparently, one who hated him bad enough to stab him in the back. In his twenties.

Evidence

Stabbed in the back. No murder weapon.

The street was super open so anyone could've run up and committed the crime then disappeared again.

No car was seen or heard at the scene, but that doesn't mean there wasn't one.

Mrs. Cruz heard a bump at the time of the murder that might've been the victim falling over.

Mia Cruz claims she didn't hear or see anything.

Nothing in the bushes.

There was a shoe at the crime scene that Mia had thrown at the victim before his death. Allegedly.

Suspects

Mia Cruz—The girlfriend who was disgruntled because Donny wouldn't propose to her. She didn't drop any hints that she knew that Donny was cheating on her with Emmy Scott. She had fought with Donny and might've had motive by virtue of that. Apparently, wanted to be a model and leave Gossip. If that was the case, why did she claim she wanted to settle down with him?

Mrs. Cruz—Tension between Mrs. Cruz and her daughter. She didn't like Donny one bit. Could she have had a motive to get rid of him because she thought he wasn't good enough for her daughter?

Noah Braxton—Noah's brother who claimed they were best friends. Could be inheriting everything from his brother, not that his brother had much that I know of. Noah's a writer so he might be struggling? That would give him an alibi. Has an alibi as he was with Emmy around the time of the murder. Need to check this.

Emmy Scott—The fiancee. Did she know about the girlfriend? If everyone in town knows, then why wouldn't she? Alibi?

I paused, tapping the nib of my stubby pencil against the page.

That was all I had so far. It wasn't much. Actually, it was a lot of questions and very few answers, and I didn't have any firm suspicions about anyone yet except for maybe Mrs. Cruz, interestingly enough.

The fact that she'd heard a noise and hadn't checked what it was, then had been the person to discover the body the next morning...

The front door of the salon opened, and I straightened, tucking my notepad and pencil away again.

Emmy Scott had emerged. She waved at the car parked behind mine, where a man with graying hair sat reading a book with his glasses perched on the edge of his nose.

I got out of the Mini and followed her.

"Miss Scott?" I called.

She stopped walking and turned to me. "Yeah? Oh, I'm sorry," she said, clutching a gaudy golden purse to her side. "I've just finished work for the day, but you can feel free to call the salon and make a booking. Ask for me directly."

"I'm not here about my hair."

She studied my short, blonde cut and arched an eyebrow. "You sure about that?"

Wow. Nice. "Yeah," I said. "I wanted to talk to you about Donny. Your fiancé?"

Emmy pressed her hand to her chest and took several breaths. The car door opened and the man inside emerged. "Honey? What's wrong? Is this woman bothering you?"

"Hi," I said, to the guy. "I'm Charlie Smith. I was just asking Miss Scott a few questions." Or I'd been about to. I circled the car and shook the man's hand. "You are?"

He wriggled his nose, the thick gray mustache beneath it moving along with it. "Mr. Scott," he said. "I'm Emmy's father. What do you want to talk to my daughter about? She's been through a lot. She doesn't need people prying into her personal life."

"I wanted to talk to her about Donny Braxton," I said. "I've been asked to—"

"Get in the car, Emmy," the father snapped, instantly. "Now. Get in the car."

Emmy gave me a miserable look and got into her father's car. She placed her purse in her lap and squeezed her eyes shut.

"I didn't mean to upset her or you," I said. "And I'm very sorry for your loss. You see, I'm a—"

"I know exactly who you are." Mr. Scott stalked forward, and I held my ground meeting him stare for stare. We were about the same height, and he didn't intimidate me one bit. Not because of the height thing, but because Gamma had taught me a wicked trick for knocking a man out with a specific finger pinch maneuver.

"Oh?"

"You're that nosy little investigator from the Gossip Inn," Mr. Scott growled. "My daughter has been through enough. She doesn't need you messing with her mind. She's finally free from that idiot's grasp, and I won't let you bring her down all over again."

"You're talking about Donny," I said. "You didn't like him."

Mr. Scott pressed his lips together.

"Mr. Scott, I'm just trying to help."

"Why? Why would you want to interfere? Let the police do their work and stay out of it. We don't need people... interfering."

He'd said that like three times in a row now. "If Emmy would like to talk to me, please give her my card." I removed a white card that I'd had printed with my name and cell phone number on it. I held it out to Mr. Scott.

He stared at it like I'd presented him with an ossified piece of poop. "Stay out of our lives. She doesn't need another stalker freak following her around." And with that, he got into his car, honked the horn at me to get me to move out of his way, then tore off. I caught a glimpse of the side of his daughter's face. It was tear-streaked.

Now, that was interesting.

In my experience, people who had secrets were the ones who didn't want others to "interfere." I hopped in the Mini-Cooper, started the engine, and set off after the Scotts.

8

The Scotts didn't go far.

They rounded the corner and entered Barkley Way, driving past double-story brick houses that were oddly familiar. No, not oddly. This was the same street that Mia and her mother lived in. What were the chances that the two women lived close to each other? Even more alarming, what were the chances that they lived on the same street?

The car passed by the Cruz residence and stopped three houses down. I pulled up behind it, leaving a gap the size of another car between us, and prepared to get out.

A feral scream rent the air.

"What on earth?" I spun around in my seat, searching for the source of the noise.

Uh oh.

Mia strode down the sidewalk toward the Scotts' car, her hands balled into fists and her gaze burning fire and brimstone.

Mr. Scott emerged from the vehicle and frowned at her.

I got out too, just in case I was needed. Though, I doubted Mr. Scott wanted me there.

"Where is she?" Mia screamed.

"Who?" Mr. Scott asked.

"I know she's here. I know it."

Emmy opened her car door and straightened. "What's going on? Oh, hey, Mia, how are you?"

The two women knew each other, at least in passing. They couldn't know each other that well, though, or they'd surely have realized they were dating the same guy.

"You cow!" Mia circled the car, grabbed hold of Emmy's blouse and tried dragging her into the road. "I'll kill you for this! I'll kill you."

Emmy released a horrified cry and tried wrenching free of the other woman's grip, but to no avail. Mia was imbued by the strength of a woman scorned, and she dug her nails in, hard.

"Let go of her!" Mr. Scott jogged into the road.

All over the street, curtains flickered or people emerged onto their porches to watch the fray. I had to admit, it was a spectacle, even for Gossip.

THE CASE OF THE SHORTCAKE SERENADE

"Calm down, everyone," I said, putting up my hands. "I'm sure we can all come to a—"

"How could you?" Mia shook Emmy this way and then that, trying to move her around but only succeeding in jiggling her on the spot. "How could you? Don't you have any shame?"

"What. Are. You. Talking. About?" Emmy gasped the words out between each successive jiggle. "Let. Go. Of. Me!"

"Young lady, unhand my daughter right this moment or I will call the police." Mr. Scott had flushed the color of Lauren's tomato jam, and he took a shaking step forward. Was it just me or did this guy look like he was about to burst into anger?

Heaven knew, the best way to diffuse a situation wasn't to add more fuel to the fire.

Finally, Emmy wrenched backward with all her might. Her blouse ripped beneath Mia's viciously sharp fingernails, leaving several long tears down the front. Emmy hugged herself and backed up, retreating to stand behind her father.

"What is the meaning of this?" Mr. Scott demanded.

"That hussy has been dating my man," Mia growled.

"What?" Mr. Scott and Emmy asked, in unison, with matching looks of disbelief.

Ah. So they didn't know about Mia. And Mia must've only just found out about Emmy. I couldn't help wondering who'd told her. Who would have lacked the common sense to do such a thing? Or maybe, it was someone who wanted to cause trouble. Always a possibility.

"My man!" Mia repeated. "You were messing around with my boyfriend, Donny."

"Donny?" Emmy sucked in a breath. "Donny's my fiancé!"

Mia recoiled as if she'd been slapped.

Oh no. This is going to be bad.

"Fiancé?" Mia asked. "Fiancé!?" She stumbled forward, going pale as a sheet. "He asked you to marry him? You of all people? Boring, ginger idiot? You're not even that pretty. You're not even anything!"

"That's enough." Mr. Scott held out an arm to protect his daughter.

"You weren't dating him," Emmy cried, tears spilling down her cheeks. "You weren't. You're lying just to hurt me, you're—"

Mia lifted a necklace bearing a heart locket and popped it open, holding it out and displaying the picture of her and Donny within, arm-in-arm. "We've been dating for months."

"Donny?" Emmy placed a hand over her mouth. "No. Why would he do this to me?"

Mr. Scott turned his back on Mia and blocked her from view, as if he could shield his daughter from the truth. "I told you he wasn't good for you, Emmy. I told you that you deserved better. No daughter of mine is—"

"Hussy!" Mia bent, ripped off her shoe, and threw it at the Scotts. It struck the back of Mr. Scott's head.

He growled under his breath and turned to his attacker, but Mia caught one look at his face then sprinted off down the road. "I'll get you for this," she cried. "I'll make you pay!"

And then she dipped into her house and slammed the door.

The silence that came after was deafening. The only sound was a dog barking somewhere in the neighborhood and the occasional chirp of a bird.

Mr. Scott herded Emmy inside before I could say a word, but not before he leveled me with a challenging stare. Yeah, maybe now wasn't the best time to talk to Emmy about her cheating fiance.

The neighbors slowly retreated, and I got into my grandmother's car and started it. A text binged through on my phone and I swiped it out of my handbag.

Meet me at the Spot as soon as you can. I've got important information about your case. Big G.

Big G was my grandmother's code name. This was great! I'd thought she wanted nothing to do with the case, or that she had more important affairs to attend to, but if she wanted to help, I couldn't be happier. I needed every bit of Intel I could get.

Something about this case didn't sit right with me. It was the parents. Both Mr. Scott and Mrs. Cruz had acted so shifty about Donny and their daughters. What did it mean?

Hopefully, Gamma would help me get to the bottom of it.

❧ 9 ❧

"The Spot" as Gamma had called it in her text was the secret underground armory beneath the inn. It never ceased to amaze me that it was under there, even though we'd spent quite a lot of time between the shelves of weapons and ammo.

I rounded the corner of the Gossip Inn, the sun shining brightly as if it wasn't the middle of winter, and reached the external basement doors painted in luminous mushrooms—that was Lauren's doing—and secured with an old-fashioned lock.

I unlocked the doors and descended into the basement, grinning excitedly at the prospect of talking to Gamma about the case. I'd missed her over the course of the past month, both because I had been busy and because she'd been... missing in action for the most part, unless she was in the kitten foster center with the cats.

The Shroom Shed—Lauren's mushroom growing project—loomed in the darkness, and I passed by it, navigating through the old junk that Gamma had stacked down here to make it seem like the basement was in disrepair.

I found the secret door on the wall, guarded by a camera that was invisible to the naked eye, and knocked once.

The lock clicked, and I entered, closing the door quickly.

Gamma sat at her touchscreen desk, wearing a frilly pink dress and a pair of cream high heels.

"You look fancy," I said.

"Goodness, do I?" Gamma glanced down at herself. "If this is fancy then I can't be putting much effort in most of the time."

I approached her. "And you smell different too."

"Charlotte, I taught you more manners than this. To comment on a person's odor?"

"I didn't say you stank or something. It's just a different perfume."

"Yes, well, that's fascinating, but I'd rather like to talk about your case," she said. "Give me a moment to bring up the relevant information, yes?"

"Right. Thanks."

While she was busy, I wandered between the rows of shelves, stopping to check out one of Gamma's new additions. A set of three egg-shaped objects that were probably grenades. They couldn't be too dangerous, as she wasn't keeping them on the pedestals in the center of the room.

Those were key-coded, guarded by misted cases and alarms so that nobody could touch them without her permission. Not that anyone knew about this place.

"What are these?" I asked, lifting one of the eggs. "Are they new?"

"Acid eggs," Gamma said, after an absent glance. "And, yes, they're new. I have a contact in Kenya who discovered a rather potent form of natural acid. Melts flesh and bone but not metal or fabric. Rather interesting technique. And potent too."

I grimaced and put the grenade down. This gave me new context as to how dangerous those pedestal items were.

"Ah, here we go," Gamma said, beckoning to me.

I joined her at the touchscreen desk.

An image of Mrs. Cruz, Mia's mother, glimmered on the screen. She held a katana upright, above her head, posing and smiling maniacally.

"What on earth? Is that a katana?"

"That is, indeed, a katana. Not made by a professional, I'm sure, but one of those mock katanas that the cosplayers use."

"Cosplayer?"

"People who like to dress up as characters from their favorite TV shows or movies. Apparently, Mrs. Cruz has quite the affection for blades."

"What's she wearing?" I asked.

"A costume, I would assume. I believe it might be something from one of those anime shows. You know, the Japanese cartoons for adults?" Gamma explained. "It doesn't prove anything, but after one of my grapes mentioned they'd seen Mrs. Cruz sneaking out of her home, I decided to do a deeper background check."

"Sneaking out? When?" I asked.

Gamma smiled at me, triumphantly. "Every Monday night at 10:00 p.m. sharp."

"That's a break in my case," I said. "She claimed that she was sleeping at that time. So, not only does she have a thing for blades, but she wasn't where she said she was and she hated the victim? It's all adding up."

"Don't get ahead of yourself, Charlotte," Gamma said, tapping away on the screen. "There's more."

"Oh?"

"I took the liberty of... plying Mr. Donny Braxton's family lawyer for information."

I didn't need to ask what she meant by that. Doubtless, that lawyer was either scarred for life or had no recollection of the interrogation my grandmother had put him through. "What did you find out?"

"That Donny was rich. Apparently, he inherited a

large sum of money from his parents. That money won't be going to his brother, Noah, but to a charity," Gamma said.

So that ruled out my money motive for Noah. Of course, it was possible that Noah might've had a different motive, but the simplest route was often the right one. "OK." I tilted my head, considering the facts.

Mrs. Cruz looked mighty suspicious to me. But what about Mr. Scott? He'd behaved aggressively about his daughter. Not protective, but downright aggressive.

"Do you have anything else you'd like me to find out for you?" Gamma asked. "I couldn't find anything on Mia other than that she was smitten with Donny."

Briefly, I told my grandmother about my encounters with Emmy and her father, Mr. Scott.

"Who, Lawrence?" Gamma asked. "Now, that is interesting. I know Lawrence has a temper, but I haven't checked out his information in my database for quite some time. Let's have a look, shall we?"

"It would be super helpful."

Gamma tapped on the desk again and an image of Mr. Scott appeared. Not just an image, but a mugshot. "Arrested three years ago for aggravated assault. And there are countless reports of domestic disturbances as far back as twenty years ago. Mr. Scott has a temper problem, as I said. Goodness, I had no idea that his temper was this bad."

"And he didn't like Donny either. He made that clear," I said.

"You said he was protective of his daughter?"

"Very," I said. "Almost angrily protective. There's something going on there, I'm not sure what."

"I think I have an inkling," Gamma said.

"Oh?"

"Mrs. Scott, Linda, she died a few years ago," Gamma said. "Car accident. Moderately suspicious at the time since there were rumors that she'd asked her husband for a divorce, but nothing ever came of it." Gamma sighed. "My best guess is that Mr. Scott is either terrified of losing his daughter, in any way shape or form, or he's worried that she knows something about his wife's death."

"Wow. That's a whole other can of worms."

"True," Gamma said. "But if he turns out to be the killer, who knows? You might wind up putting him away for two crimes instead of one."

I bit down on the inside of my lip and considered it. "I'd like to do some recon tonight," I said. "Get into the Cruz house and take a look around. Find out if Mrs. Cruz is keeping weapons in there, and if so, whether they were perhaps used at the crime scene."

"Good idea," Gamma said. "I'll meet you here at eight 'o'clock sharp."

I did a little salute, a half-habit, half-joke, then left

my grandmother to enjoy her alone time among her weapons, many of which were pretty darn illegal, and high-tech gadgets. I wanted to help Lauren at least a little today. That way I could keep the guilt over neglecting my duties at bay.

❧ 10 ❧

That night...

I checked my phone again and sighed. It was fifteen minutes past eight and my grandmother was nowhere to be found. She hadn't come to the back of the inn to meet me before suit up for our reconnaissance mission, and it wasn't like I had a key for her armory so I could do the mission on my own.

Not that I would even consider barging into her private armory when she wasn't around.

Lauren was right.

My grandmother had never been late for anything in her life. She'd once joked that the only thing she'd be late

64

for was her own funeral. She planned on living until the ripe old age of 110.

This was beyond unusual.

I typed out a text, quickly.

We were meant to meet fifteen minutes ago. Is everything OK?

I waited, frowning. The text message came through seconds later.

Sorry, Chaplin. Something came up. I'll explain later. Big G.

And that was it.

I huffed out a breath into the quiet night and tucked my phone into my pocket. What was I meant to do about this? I couldn't go ahead and do recon without her. I didn't have the night vision contact lenses, and I would've preferred having Gamma by my side for this.

Grow up. Just go out there and find out the truth.

I had lost my patience waiting around for information, and I was far more impulsive than my grandmother. Besides, I had my date with Detective Goode tomorrow night. If there was ever a time to do something irrational that would get me in trouble, now was it.

I made a snap decision and strode off around the side of the Gossip Inn, the gravel crunching underfoot. I passed by the kitchen and the small greenhouse where Quinton and his gorgeous dog, Charlie, worked and rounded the front of the inn.

My grandmother's Mini-Cooper was still parked out front, which made things even more interesting.

If she wasn't at the inn, where was she? The inn was slightly removed from Gossip, so it would be tough to walk anywhere far. Had someone picked her up? Or was she somewhere close-by?

It didn't matter right this second, and it certainly wouldn't help me solve the case.

I grabbed Gamma's car keys from inside then got into the Mini-Cooper and headed off.

❦

THE CRUZ HOUSEHOLD WAS ALIGHT, THE WINDOW upstairs open as it had been the last time I'd stopped by. I had parked the Mini across the street under a tree, and I watched the house idly, tapping my fingers on the steering wheel.

This thing with Gamma bugged me, but I had to focus up. I couldn't do anything about her absence now except talk to her when I saw her again.

Mia appeared in the upstairs window, briefly, holding her cellphone to her ear and gesturing wildly. She disappeared out of view.

The front door was ajar downstairs, allowing a sliver of light onto the porch from within, and the curtains in the living room were open as well. Mrs. Cruz sat watching TV, occasionally lifting the remote to change the channel.

But everything she'd watched in the last fifteen minutes was a news report.

Interesting that she was so obsessed with the news. She would flick through the channels constantly, almost as if she was waiting for something.

She's looking for a report about Donny's death. I'd bet my last slice of shortcake.

It amazed me how open everyone was in Gossip. Of course, they had no reason to mistrust anyone since it was a tiny, safe town. But the fact that these two were so relaxed was intriguing. A man had been killed in their front yard and they left the door open? Not just unlocked, but open? Weird. Or suspicious.

What would Gamma think of this?

I got out of the Mini and went up to the house. I knocked on the front door, loudly. "Hello?"

"Who's there?" Mrs. Cruz yelped from within. "Who is that?"

"It's Charlie," I said. "Charlie Smith. The fixer?"

"Oh right, come on in."

I entered the house, hoping that this wasn't a grave mistake on my part. If I was too brash about this, I might get in a lot of trouble.

Mrs. Cruz sat on the couch in the living room. She'd switched off the TV and turned to me, offering a hollow smile. "Hello, Miss Smith," she said. "I'm glad to see you. Have you come with an update?"

"Unfortunately, I don't have one yet, but I do have a couple of questions for you. I think you might be able to help me figure this out and clear your daughters name."

"All right. Please, sit down."

I remained standing. It would make her uncomfortable that I'd refused her hospitality, and it would make her tense and more likely to become emotional when I confronted her.

"Did you tell your daughter about Emmy Scott?" I asked.

Mrs. Cruz stared at me, frozen like a statue.

"Because there was an altercation earlier today."

"I... well, it wasn't that I told her so much. Rather, it was that I heard about it and I was talking to my friend on the phone when she overheard me."

"I see." *So, she happened to be talking about such a sensitive topic in the house? Where Mia could easily overhear?* Not buying that. "Tell me, Mrs. Cruz, why did you lie to me about where you were on Monday night?"

This was possibly the most impulsive thing I'd done, and that was saying a lot, but I needed answers, and thought I believed that Mrs. Cruz wanted to help her daughter, I wasn't convinced of her innocence.

"W-what? I told you the truth."

"Really. Because I've learned that you leave at 10:00

p.m. every Monday night. And that you enjoy using katanas. Is that correct?"

"H-how did you—? Where? I don't understand."

Finally, I took a seat, so that our eyes were level. "I'm not trying to frighten you, Mrs. Cruz. I need you to understand that I want to be on your side, but if you really want me to clear your daughter's name, you're going to have to tell me the truth."

Mrs. Cruz gulped audibly. "I didn't want anyone to know."

"Why?"

"Because they... it's not normal."

"What isn't?"

"What I do. It's not normal."

"What is it that you do every Monday evening, Mrs. Cruz?" I asked.

"I go to... I have a meeting."

"What kind of meeting?"

"Mayclu," Mrs. Cruz whispered.

"Mayclu?"

"Anime club!" She covered her face with both hands. "I go to anime club. That's where I was on Monday night. You can check it out if you don't believe me. I didn't touch that man, I just didn't want anyone to know where I was, OK?'

"So, those things you told me about the night of the murder weren't true? You didn't hear a bump?" I asked.

"No," she said.

"But how did you not see the body when you got home from anime club?" I asked.

"Because I only got back the next morning, right when I told you I found the body. I sleep over at a hotel when I go to club because we all dress up, and I don't want people to see me leaving the house in my costume," she sighed. "Everything else I told you was the truth, I swear. But I wasn't here on Monday night. You can check."

And I would have to.

If what she'd said was true, I could rule Mrs. Cruz out as a suspect entirely.

❧ 11 ❧

The following evening...

I t should've been criminal to be this nervous. It wasn't as if I'd never been on a date before, but this was different.

Aaron Goode drove me up the wall. He made me angrier than I'd ever been with a man before, and I wasn't sure if that was because we were so similar personality-wise or if he was just *that annoying.* But if he was that annoying, I would never have agreed to go on a date with him in the first place.

A part of me really liked the guy.

Besides, this date would distract me from Gamma's

absence today and her dodging my questions about why she hadn't gone on the recon mission with me last night.

I exhaled slowly and checked my reflection in the mirror over my dressing table.

Sunlight and Cocoa Puff sat on my bed, watching with varying degrees of interest as I studied my reflection.

I had chosen a pair of jeans and a silk blouse. A nice change from my usual pair of jeans and t-shirt look. I had thrown on some makeup, styled my hair, and even spritzed on perfume and borrowed a golden bracelet from Lauren. More like she'd forced it on me.

I'd taken the bracelet as a concession to get her to not try to style my hair in a fantastic beehive. How she thought she'd get that right with my thin blonde locks was another question entirely.

"You can do this," I said to my reflection, pointing. "It will be fine."

This morning, I had called the leader of the anime club and found out that Mrs. Cruz was, indeed, telling the truth. She met with them at a hotel in the town over where they would gather, dressed up as their favorite characters, and discuss the show they were watching.

When I'd asked about the show itself, he'd yelled, "Subs before dubs!" Whatever that meant.

Regardless, I could officially cross Mrs. Cruz off my suspect list.

A good thing.

I gave each of the kitties a kiss then exited my bedroom and started down the stairs. Detective Goode had said he would pick me up in the foyer.

This was silly. I should've been calling him Aaron at this point, but it felt like... I would be giving something up if I did. That didn't make much sense, but oh well.

Goode was in the foyer as promised, looking dapper in a buttoned-down long sleeve shirt and a pair of jeans. The scent of his cologne drifted over, and I swallowed, offering him a smile that I hoped didn't come across as too nervous.

"Smith," he said. "You look great."

"Such a charmer," I replied, sarcastically.

"Uh oh. What did I do?"

"Nothing," I said, relaxing my shoulders. "You look good too."

"You hear that?" Goode asked, cupping a hand to his ear. "That's the sound of pigs flying. I can't believe you just complimented me."

"Don't start," I replied, laughing.

The ice was officially broken.

Goode and I kept a respectable distance from each other and headed out into the night. I got into his car, a white hatchback, and we drove off. Goode hit the button for the stereo and music flooded the car.

"So," he said, "I know there isn't much to choose

from in this town, food-wise. Did you have anywhere in mind?"

"The most popular place is the Hungry Steer."

"Oh yeah? I've been there a couple of times," he said. "The burgers are pretty good."

"Burgers sound great." My stomach actually grumbled, and I blushed. What the heck? I never blushed about food. Food was one of the great joys of life. Food and cats.

We drove in nervous silence to the Hungry Steer.

Goode leaped out of the car, raced around to my side, and opened the door for me.

"You didn't have to do that," I said.

"I wanted to." A warm smile parted his lips, and the butterflies in my stomach decided to put on a gymnastic performance.

Oh boy, was I in trouble with this guy.

We entered the Hungry Steer, with its country Christmas music, hay bales, and cute booths with red vinyl seats, and took a place near the back. Not too close to the bathroom or kitchen doors, but close enough. It was a Friday night, and the place was busy enough. Heads turned, intrigued gazes wandered our way.

I'd banked on people gossiping, but yeah, I was pretty sure my date with Goode would be headline news by tomorrow morning.

An elderly woman nearby removed her phone from

her purse and began typing away frantically, glancing at us every few taps of her thumbs on the screen.

Make that headline news within the hour.

A server sidled over to us and took our order, root beer and two bacon burgers with fries, and then we were alone.

"So," I said, "how was your day?"

"Good," he replied, easily. "Good as it can be when I've got a murder case."

"I heard about that."

"Oh? I bet you did." Goode laughed. "You've heard about every case I've been involved in."

I didn't blush about that at all. "That's... well."

"Well?"

Did I say it outright? He would find out anyway, wouldn't he? Surely, the rumors about me being a problem fixer had already reached his ears. But to tell him that that was what I wanted to do as a job?

"Nothing."

"Go ahead," Goode said. "I can tell you want to say something important."

Was it important? *It's only your future, Charlie.*

A future that I had yet to discuss with Gamma because she was never around these days. Right before Christmas too.

"I'm a fixer," I said, blurting it out.

"Huh? Like... a handywoman?"

"No," I laughed. "I'm sure you've heard the rumors about me around town, but yeah. I help people by fixing their problems. They hire me to find out the truth about things, or if they've lost something to find it, that kind of thing. That's why you think I've been involved in your cases. I was just doing my job."

"Right." He glanced away, irritably.

"What?"

"Nothing, it's just that that job already exists. It's called being a law enforcement official."

"That's not entirely true," I said. "I do things that officers can't."

"You mean that you break the law."

Openly hostile on a date. Nice.

"OK," I said. "If that's how you want to see it. I help people."

"By breaking the law."

I glared at him, burning hot all over. "Are you good? You're being kind of rude."

"I'm being rude," he said. "Sure. I'm the one being rude. Do you know what your problem is, Charlotte? You think that you can do whatever you want, whenever you want, without consequence. You act like you know better than everyone else. Than the police. That's the reason you got arrested not so long ago."

"Excuse me, but last we spoke, you thanked me for helping you," I said. "Where's the gratitude now?"

He opened his mouth to respond, but I shoved up from the table and slipped out of the booth.

"Forget I asked," I said. "This was a mistake, Goode. Don't bother asking me out again because I won't say yes." And with that, I marched from the Hungry Steer, hunger forgotten and shame burning hot in the corners of my eyes.

❧ 12 ❧

The following morning...

"I'm telling you, Charlie, I don't like it," Lauren said, as she chopped bacon into itty bitty pieces at the counter. "She keeps disappearing. She's meant to be here this morning, but she's not, and that's not like her."

I didn't comment. I happened to agree with Lauren about my grandmother's suspicious behavior, but I struggled to focus on it right now. Last night's date had been an unmitigated disaster.

What was worse, a lot of what Detective Goode had said to me had rung true. But it was made bitter by the fact that he was clearly angry I was stepping on his toes.

I got that. He had job security to worry about, but at the same time, not every one of my clients would come forward with a murder investigation.

"Charlie?"

"Yeah. Sorry." I pulled my ski goggles down and lifted my onion cutting knife. I had promised I would chop onions for her this morning after being absent for the past couple of weeks.

"No, it's not the onions," she said. "I was just wondering what you thought about—"

My grandmother swept into the kitchen, and Lauren rammed her teeth together so hard that they clicked.

"Good morning," Gamma said.

"Hello, Georgina." Lauren's tone was almost aloof. She wiped her hands off on her apron and raised both red eyebrows at her employer. "How are you?"

"Busy," Gamma replied. "Unfortunately, I won't be able to help you two with breakfast. I've got to check on the cats." My grandmother wore a gorgeous cream lace dress today with matching heels, and she smelled distinctly of that fancy perfume. She looked far too fancy for the pale green kitchen with its ticking clock above the door.

Even Cocoa Puff, Sunlight, and Snowy stared at her like they'd never seen her before.

"I'm sure you can handle the guests. It's awfully quiet this time of year," Gamma said.

"Sure, we can," I said, lifting my ski goggles onto my forehead. "But I was hoping to catch up with you, Georgina. We have a few things to discuss."

"Yes, of course. But that will have to wait, I'm afraid. The cats." And with that, she swept out of the kitchen and headed off down the hallway.

I glanced at Lauren. The chef gave a frantic nod.

Quick as I could, I stripped off the ski goggles and chased after my grandmother, my footsteps quiet. I reached the hall just as the connecting door to the kitten foster center and cat hotel clicked closed. I waited a few seconds then followed her in, unlocked the door with my thick, bronze key.

Inside, Gamma had already reached the other end of the center and was at the back doors. She opened one, careful not to allow the kittens to escape, and stepped out into the sunshine.

I raced after her, my pulse ticking upward with every step.

She was up to something, and I could find out what it was right here and now. Life wasn't the same without my grandmother helping me with cases or gracing us with her presence in the kitchen. And Gamma was classy, but she wasn't "lace dress and high heels" classy.

I followed her out into the inn's grounds. She circled the building, and I followed, careful not to walk on the gravel or alert her of my presence. Gamma moved swiftly past the closed kitchen door and around the front of the inn.

There a black, sleek BMW awaited her. She got into the passenger side, and the car drove off.

What on earth? Where is she going?

I darted inside, grabbed the Mini-Cooper keys, and let myself into my grandmother's car. Why hadn't she taken it instead of getting a ride from some stranger in a luxury car? It didn't make sense.

I started the engine and raced after her, banking on the driver of Gamma's car not having any advanced driving experience. I kept my distance, making sure that I hung at least three cars back at all times, and following them into town.

It was no mean feat to avoid notice. My grandmother was switched on. She was always on the lookout for danger because she had so many incredibly dangerous enemies, but the black BMW didn't swerve or act erratically. Nor did it try to lose me.

Finally, it drove through the center of Gossip and into a side alleyway, where it parked in front of...

My heart dropped.

I parked the Mini-Cooper in an open spot in Main Street, then hopped out of the car, suddenly sweaty all over. I wiped my hands off on my apron and raced to the corner of 2nd Avenue, peering down to where the BMW had parked.

The man who had emerged from the car had silver hair and wore a white coat. A doctor's coat. He opened the door for my grandmother and offered her a hand. She emerged from within, dipping her head and smiling pleasantly, not at all worried that she might be being observed.

Heavens, she didn't even do her cursory scan of the street or surrounding buildings.

Instead, the man guided her toward the glass front door of the building and opened it. They entered together and the door shut again, affording me a view of the words printed across the front.

Doctor Puddles, G.P.

Was my grandmother sick?

13

I waited impatiently on the street corner, my gut churning.

It was the unthinkable that my grandmother might be ill. She was a rock. A constant in Gossip and in my life, and the only stability I'd had in the years after my divorce from my murderous ex-husband. What would Lauren do? Or the cats? The inn?

Breathe, Charlotte. You don't know what's going on yet.

I stood on the corner, angry that I hadn't spent enough time with her this week. It wasn't just that I was kind of stuck with my case at the moment, it was that if she was ill...

The front door of the doctor's practice opened, and my grandmother emerged with the doctor in tow. They made for the black BMW again, but this time, I didn't hide. Instead, I set off across the road to intercept them.

"Georgina," I called, as I crossed the street.

My grandmother halted, her eyes widening. A flicker of anger passed her features, but I doubted it had anything to do with me. If I knew Gamma, she was mad at herself for not having realized I was following her.

I stopped on the sidewalk beside her and the doctor.

"Hello," I said to him. "Can I talk to you for a second?" That was directed at my grandmother.

"Of course, Charlotte." She smiled at the doctor. "You'll have to excuse me, Nathan. I need to attend to some important business. We'll talk again soon."

Gamma was on a first name basis with her doctor?

She accompanied me back across the road, nodding to the friendly residents we passed on the sidewalk. Finally, we were in the Mini-Cooper again, me in the driver's seat.

I turned to my grandmother immediately. "Why didn't you tell me?" I asked. "What was the point of hiding it from me? Lauren's been worried sick about you, you know and—"

"Oh, Charlotte, please. Do you really think running me on a guilt trip about my personal life is going to work? I'm a grown woman."

"Yeah, and we care about you. I'm your... you know." I didn't say granddaughter out loud because it might blow her cover or mine. "We're practically family." Literally

84

family, but it slipped out easier. "You can't ignore us. You owe us some kind of explanation."

"I don't owe anyone anything." Gamma folded her arms, primly. "Goodness, but you're being unreasonable. You'd think I had a terminal illness."

I blinked. "Wait, what?"

"Just the way you're acting about. It's as if I have a terminal illness and I didn't tell you."

"Don't you?"

"What?" It was Gamma's turn to look completely puzzled.

"You... you're at the doctor's office," I said. "You've been missing over the past few months. I assumed that there had to be something seriously wrong with your health when I saw you go in there. You're not sick?"

"Sick?" Gamma crossed herself. "Goodness me, no. Thank goodness, I mean. I'm blessed in that I'm in good health."

"Then why on earth were you..." I trailed off. "Oh."

What kind of doctor would pick up one his patients at her home? And why on earth would he have opened the door for her? Gamma wore perfume, and a gorgeous dress, and she'd been styling her hair differently of late. She was always busy and definitely avoiding talking to us.

"You're dating Doctor Puddles?"

"Shush." But Gamma went rosy pink. "Now, don't say that too loud. You know, we've been trying to be discreet.

It's difficult to hide anything in this town, as you well know, and we're just not ready to discuss it with everyone else."

"Oh." Thank goodness it was just a romantic thing. "Oh wait, so you blew me off the other night to go out with the doctor."

Gamma bowed her head. "Now, I felt terrible about that, but I just... he had an appointment on short notice during our previous date, so that was the only time we could see each other. It was unplanned. I'm sorry about that Charlotte."

"No, that's OK. I'm just glad I know what's going on. You're going to have to tell Lauren, though. She's worried sick."

"If I tell Lauren, she'll tell everyone," Gamma said.

"You're that shy?"

"I don't want Nathan to feel embarrassed."

"His name is Doctor Puddles," I replied. "He could have his own kids TV show. I'm pretty sure the embarrassment thing is not an issue for him."

Gamma gave a giggle. An actual giggle. "I'm just not used to this type of thing, you know. I would much rather keep him a secret. What if he gets embroiled in my affairs?"

By affairs she meant her past as a spy.

"Oh, Charlotte, it's been so long since I've done anything like this. Dating? It's terrifying. I thought for sure that I was done with dating, but Nathan is so sweet. He buys me flowers and treats me like a lady. He's interested in what I have to say, and he has a wicked sense of humor. I like him. A lot."

"Then go for it," I said. "Don't be afraid. If you really want to, we can kidnap him, blindfold him, swear him to secrecy under threat of death, and then tell him about your past?"

"You're too sweet." Gamma patted my knee. "But I think I'll do that in my own time, in the old fashioned way. Verbally. Without guns."

"That *is* old fashioned."

Gamma gave me broad grin. "I've been so neglectful. Can you forgive me, Charlotte?"

"There's nothing to forgive," I said. "I'm just happy that you're OK. And that you're happy." I wriggled my lips from side-to-side. "Although, I could use your help."

"The case?"

"Yeah. I'm stuck."

"Tell me all about it," Gamma said, sitting back in her seat and growing serious.

❧ 14 ❧

"**S**o," Gamma said, "you've got an alibi for Mrs. Cruz, but not for Mia, Emmy, Mr. Scott, or the brother."

"I kind of have an alibi for Emmy and the brother, but I can't actually prove it because I can't talk to Emmy at all," I said. "Her father's protecting her."

Gamma wriggled her nose from side-to-side, considering.

"I don't get why he would need to protect her unless he's got something to hide?"

Another nose wriggle.

"You have, effectively, a crime scene that doesn't exist since you never saw it, no murder weapon, hardly any alibis, and barely a lead. Short of breaking into every suspects house, which we could do, you don't have anything."

"And even if I did break into every suspect's house," I said, "there's no guarantee I'll find the evidence I need. It's not like there was any surveillance footage."

"Surveillance footage." Gamma's sentence came out as a murmur. "Surveillance footage."

"What is it?"

"Just a thought. You mentioned earlier in the week that you spoke to Josie about the shortcake that was found at the scene, correct?" Gamma asked.

"Yes. And she told me that the victim picked up a box of shortcake every Monday without fail."

"But where did he go after?" Gamma asked. "Did Josie say anything about that?"

I wracked my brain.

"Oh." It hit me fast as lightning. "Yeah, she did. She told me that Donny exited The Little Cake Shop and turned left on the sidewalk, heading toward The Hungry Steer."

"Start the car," Gamma said.

I did, immediately, clipping on my seatbelt. "The Hungry Steer?"

"Grayson Tombs is as miserly as they come. If anyone's going to have surveillance cameras it's him, especially after the issues he had with his son."

That felt like years ago. Technically it had been. "Then to the Hungry Steer we go. Though, I don't know that the footage will help. It's not like we'll see him being stabbed."

Then again, any lead was good at this point. The truth was, as much as I'd loved investigating the case, asking questions of the suspects and so on, I was stuck in another way.

Stuck on how I felt about my interaction with Goode on our date, stuck on leaving the inn. After the scare I'd just had with my grandmother, how could I possibly do that? How would life ever be the same when I wasn't living in the Gossip Inn?

"Charlotte, you do realize we actually have to drive down the road to get to the Hungry Steer, don't you?" My grandmother's whip-sharp tone brought me back down to Earth with a bump.

"Right," I said, grinning.

I banished the negative, confused thoughts for another time. Today, we had a case to solve, and finally, I had my grandmother on my side.

"AND WHY SHOULD I TALK TO YOU ABOUT ANYTHING related to a murder case?" Grayson Tombs sat behind his massive walnut desk in his office at the Hungry Steer, looking like the cat who'd caught the fattest of rats.

"Because it's right thing to do, Mr. Tombs," Gamma said.

And my grandmother will incapacitate you if you don't. But of course Gamma wouldn't do that to an upstanding citizen of Gossip. At least not where anyone could see. Or where he could scream and alert anyone.

"I haven't talked to you in years," Tombs said, pressing his lips outward like a little fountain. "I don't feel like starting now."

"I've got to be honest with you, Mr. Tombs," Gamma said, "I don't quite give a flying rat's butt what you do or don't feel like doing. Your happiness is the least of my concerns."

Tombs pressed himself backward in his fancy leather chair, so far back that he grew double chins and looked as if he was an astronaut under severe G-force.

"What I care about, Mr. Tombs, is finding out what happened to a member of our upstanding society."

Tombs cleared his throat and relaxed a little. "I would hardly call Donny Braxton an upstanding member of our society. Not Gossip society." Tombs had a very gently twang to his accent. An affectation, I was sure.

"I should extend the list of things I don't care about to what you think," Gamma said.

"You're being awful rude, Georgina. Haven't you heard the saying that you'll catch more flies with honey?"

"I only have the patience to swat flies."

"Is that a threat?"

"I don't make threats," Gamma said, in that dangerous, quiet tone. The one that made most men jerk themselves straight before she corrected them forcibly.

Oh man, that Doctor Puddles has no idea what he's gotten himself into.

"Why should I show you my surveillance footage? Why shouldn't I take it to the police?" Grayson smirked.

Gamma got up from her chair so suddenly, even I started.

She circled the desk, keeping her gaze on Grayson every step of the way, her heels clacking on the wooden boards.

"Mr. Tombs," she said. "I'm going to give you a final opportunity to do as I've asked."

Oh, this wouldn't end well. I didn't question my grandmother here. She was getting appropriately serious given the situation, and if I was honest, Mr. Tombs had it coming. Before Lauren had had her first son, Tyke, Mr. Tombs had been obsessed with her. He'd made her highly uncomfortable. He'd demanded to see her and bothered us at the inn.

"I won't bow to a little old lady's threats," Grayson said.

"Charlotte."

That was all I needed. I got up from my squeaky

chair—much less impressive than Grayson's—and moved to the office door. I locked it.

"What on earth are you doing?" Grayson asked. "Unlock that door, right now."

Gamma reached the back of his chair. She extended two fingers and pressed them into his neck. He stiffened, still conscious, his eyes wide and staring directly ahead.

"You won't remember this when you wake up, Mr. Tombs," Gamma said. "I want you to know that this was a necessity, but I do take pleasure in it."

I grinned at my grandmother. Honestly, this was pretty terrifying for Tombs. He didn't know what was about to happen.

"I'm going to direct you, and you're going to do as I say, do you understand?" Gamma shifted slightly. "Raise your hand if you understand."

Tombs raised his hands.

"Wonderful. Now, open your laptop and locate the surveillance footage."

"You're not worried he'll yell?" I asked.

"He can't," she replied.

I didn't bother asking. My grandmother had studied every martial art form known to man and several that weren't. Tombs would have to do exactly as she asked.

And he did. He opened his laptop and navigated to the surveillance footage, inputting passwords where necessary. Gamma found the correct day of footage and sent it directly to her burner email address, then had him delete the email.

"Now," she said, removing a tiny pill from her ring. "You're going to crush this between your teeth. When you wake up, you won't remember anything. I want you to know, Mr. Tombs, that I abhor the way you treated my chef, but your business is quite well-run." She inserted the pill between his teeth, released the grip on his neck, then forced his teeth closed like he was a particularly stubborn cat being fed medicine.

Grayson passed out before he could call out for help.

"He runs his business quite well?" I asked.

"I like to end an interrogation with a compliment," Gamma said. "It feels polite. Especially when I'm taking information from a person against their will. Now, do you really want to hang around talking about that, or do you want to find out who murdered Donny Braxton?"

❦ 15 ❦

amma and I entered the armory in a rush, both excited. Me because I was close to solving the case, or rather, I was closer than I'd been a couple of hours ago. Her because she'd told me about Doctor Puddles and wouldn't have to sneak around anymore.

"You know, I still can't quite believe how relaxed I was," Gamma said. "I should've noticed you following us."

"Too busy flirting with your doctor boyfriend, eh?"

"Stop it, Charlotte, I'm serious."

"Are you kidding me? After all the times you teased me about my love life?" I asked. "No shot am I letting you get away with this."

Gamma flapped a hand at me then took her favorite spot in the armory, on her comfy leather stool in front of her touchscreen desk. She tapped away until she found the email in question then downloaded the video footage we'd taken from Grayson Tombs.

"He's really not going to remember anything?" I asked.

"No," Gamma said, confidently. "And a pity too because he'll still treat me like a little old woman as he put it. The older I get, the more I realize that age is a mindset."

"And that big mouths get people in trouble."

"Precisely. Grayson Tombs has a mouth that could swallow a blue whale."

I snorted a laugh.

Gamma gestured for me to bring a chair over, and I fetched it from further along the desk. It felt so good to be chatting and laughing again. My grandmother and I were on the same wavelength. I doubted I'd ever make a friend like her.

Yet you're planning leaving the inn?

"All right," Gamma said, trawling through the footage. "Let's see what we've got here."

We moved through the footage carefully over the next hour, searching for any sign of Donny on the way past the Hungry Steer. It was a long shot, but we had to take any lead we could get, and Josie had said that he'd gone in that direction.

Unless, of course, she'd been lying to mess with me. I wouldn't put it past her, honestly.

"There," Gamma said. "That's Donny Braxton." She pointed to a figure onscreen and slowed down the footage significantly. He was tall and handsome, with sandy brown hair. He held a box in his hand that had to be the shortcake.

"There he goes," I said, and my heart sank. It wasn't exactly groundbreaking footage. Sure the guy had walked past on the way to see his girlfriend, but it wasn't like he'd gone past particularly late in the day.

The timestamp said that Donny had passed the Hungry Steer at around seven in the evening, which was probably right after the bakery had closed its doors. But that didn't help us—

"Who's that?" I pointed.

Across the street, another figure came into view. Someone tall, wearing a dark hoodie. They followed Donny down the street and they were...

"Limping," I said. "He's limping."

"Goodness, Charlotte," Gamma replied, "you can't just assume that's a man because the person is tall."

"I'm not assuming. I know who that is."

"Oh?"

I smiled at my grandmother, triumphantly. "That's Donny's brother, Noah. I met him earlier in the week, and he's the only suspect who walks with a limp."

"Interesting."

"Now, we just have to figure out why he was following Donny," I said. "He claimed that he was with Emmy at the time of the murder, but this footage doesn't prove he was lying. It's too early in the evening. And I can't exactly reach out to Mr. Scott or Emmy and ask them. They'll shut me out."

"Then we know what we have to do," Gamma said. "It's time for that recon mission I missed out on earlier in the week."

And just like that, I had my grandmother back.

THE TASK NOW WAS TO EITHER PROVE OR DISPROVE THE brother's involvement. The trouble was, I had no idea why Noah would've wanted to get rid of his brother. It didn't add up.

He didn't need money, since he was a romance novelist and his parents had left him plenty of it, and not only that, he hadn't inherited any of it from Donny, anyway. We had to be missing something, right?

Some crucial piece of evidence that would lead us to the real killer, but without a body, a murder weapon, and just witness testimony to go on, this was tough.

Even Mrs. Cruz had lied to me about her alibi, though it had been seriously risky to do so.

"We need direct physical evidence," Gamma said. "Or proof that he was where he said he was. Are you reading me, Chaplin?"

"Loud and clear." I whispered it, the flesh-colored microphone at my throat picking up the tiniest vibrations.

My grandmother was in the car, watching through the pinhole camera attached to my lapel. We had stopped down the street from Noah's house, and I had gone on alone, wearing the black armor that my grandmother had specially ordered for me from one of her contacts.

"If necessary, I can send in the FlyBoy Drone with a teensy little bomb on it," Gamma said.

"You've been feeling trigger happy of late, haven't you?"

"I deny all allegations."

I slinked past the pink flamingo out front and along the side of the house, breathing easily, aware that if anyone saw me, outfit complete with my balaclava, they would call the cops for sure. And I definitely wouldn't have that.

The windows along the side of the house were open, the lights off inside, but there was someone awake in the house. Noah hummed inside, tapping away on an obnoxious-sounding mechanical keyboard.

I stopped beneath a window, listening.

There was no chance he would hear me break-in. I

wouldn't even need to break in, technically. The window was open wide. Sure, Christmas hadn't been exactly cold, but it wasn't like we were in the middle of a heat wave. What was with everyone leaving their doors or windows open in Gossip.

Not that I can complain.

"I'm going in," I breathed.

"I'll be watching, Chaplin."

I hoisted myself through the window and into the room beyond. It was a darkened bedroom, carpeted, thankfully, and light spilled into it from the hallway beyond. I proceeded toward the door and peered out.

The hall ended in a study where Noah sat wearing headphones and typing away happily. Every so often he would stop and chuckle at something he'd written or mutter, "That's great!"

At least he was confident. But was he a killer?

I shut the door, grateful for the night vision contact lenses that bathed the room in a green hue. The king-sized bed against the wall was neatly made, but the sheets themselves were fancy for a small home in a lower middle class area.

If Noah the novelist was so well-off, why was he living here?

The typing continued, and I moved to the bedside table and slid the drawer open. A diary lay within.

Bingo.

Or it had no information in it, and I was totally out of luck. I flipped the book open and... empty. Who kept an empty diary in their bedroom?

I shut it, frowning, and returned it to its hidey hole.

Think, Charlotte, think.

He hadn't wanted money. He had been friends with Emmy. He... *he had been friends with Emmy.*

I blinked. There was something there. Romance novelist. Friends with Emmy. Jealousy? Shortcake for Emmy?

My mind whirred.

I was onto something, I could feel it.

I moved to the other side of the bed and slid that desk drawer open. A picture frame, lying upside down slid into view. I extracted it, pausing to listen for the sound of Noah's keyboard, and turned it over.

The image in the frame was bathed in green light thanks to my contacts.

"Interesting," Gamma said, in my ear. "That's Emmy Scott, isn't it?"

"Yes," I whispered.

The words Mr. Scott had said to me when we'd first met, on the day when I'd waited for Emmy outside of the salon came back. *"She doesn't need another stalker freak following her around."*

He hadn't meant her fiancé.

The image was a picture of Emmy and Noah, the

romance novelist, laughing hysterically at something. Donny hovered in the background, watching.

But it wasn't Donny who was the stalker freak.

Was it that simple? Had Noah really murdered his own brother for love?

"Chaplin," my grandmother said. "Are you reading me?"

"Loud and clear, Big G."

"The cops are coming down the road."

I heard the sirens seconds after she'd said it, and my heart leaped into my throat. Obviously, Goode had information I didn't. The body, the evidence at the crime scene, leads I didn't have access to. He'd figured out that it was, indeed, the brother who'd done it.

I could slink off now. Let him take credit. I could—

The typing in the kitchen stopped. A chair scraped and uneven footsteps thumped down the hall toward the bedroom door.

It was Noah, trying to make a hasty escape.

"Hurry," Gamma said.

"You go," I replied.

"Chaplin!"

"Go," I breathed.

The door opened, and Noah stumbled into the room, clicked on the light and stopped dead, wide-eyed, staring at me. He was pale as a sheet.

"Hi," I said, pleasantly, and then, with very little

finesse by my grandmother's standards. I punched him on the jaw so hard, he passed out on the spot with a thumping of legs and arms.

"Nice punch," Gamma said. "Now get out of there."

"No," I said. "I want him to know I'm serious."

"You'll get in trouble."

"For what?" I asked, stripping off my balaclava and shoving it into my back pocket. "I'll say I heard a noise. A scream. That I came running and I found him trying to escape."

"You're wearing armor."

"They don't know that. It looks like plain black clothing," I said.

Gamma sighed. "I don't like this."

But it was too late to turn back now.

The front door burst open. Thumping and shouts, the police announcing themselves came next.

"In here," I shouted.

Detective Goode burst into the room, leading the other officers, and they all pulled up short.

I smiled at him, triumphantly. "It's about time you got here."

❧ 16 ❧

In a stunning turn of events, I was a free woman.

I hadn't been arrested because of my excuse and because I'd stopped Noah from escaping the house before the police got there. He'd had a bag packed and ready to go and had used the last of his inheritance from his parents to buy two plane tickets to Puerto Rico.

The police theorized he'd planned on taking Emmy with him, whether she wanted to go or not. Creepy.

Regardless, I had made it through another investigation, even if this one definitely hadn't gone as planned.

I sat on the porch swing, Sunlight in my lap, and took a breather. So much had happened over the past week that I needed it.

My grandmother exited onto the porch and leaned against the doorjamb. "You know, he's not going to stop calling."

"I'm not ready to talk to him yet." Goode had been trying to get hold of me all week. And I'd been successfully ignoring him.

I'd pretty clearly declared my intent to become Gossip's fixer by capturing the killer, and I didn't care what he thought about it. I didn't want to hear the apology yet, if there was one, and I wasn't ready to talk about it.

"I just want to focus on the future," I said. "I was thinking about Christmas. And after Christmas."

"After Christmas?" Gamma asked.

"Yes," I said. "I think... I want to stop working here. At the inn. I'm going to try to find a place of my own and start my business as a fixer for the town. I don't want to put any financial strain on you, though. If you need me here then—"

"Oh, Charlotte, please," Gamma laughed. "All you do is dust on occasion and entertain the cats. I've been secretly looking for a second assistant."

"Wow."

"No offense."

"None taken," I said. "I haven't exactly been the best assistant around."

Gamma sat down on the porch swing beside me, smiling at Sunlight who purred at her and demanded a few head scratches. "The best assistant?" Gamma asked. "No, not that. But you have been and always will be the best granddaughter a woman could ask for."

It was such a rare occurrence that she would break cover, even in private, that I welled up.

"You're not too bad yourself, Gamma," I whispered.

She squeezed my hand once then released it and got up. "Well, if you plan on leaving the inn in the New Year, I've got to plan something extra special for Christmas."

"Like what?"

"How about a getaway?" Gamma asked. "Somewhere cold and snowy. Where Goode can't find you. Where there's no cell phone service so he can't phone you either. Or me for that matter." She clicked her tongue and drew her phone from the pocket of her apron. She showed me the screen. "Speak of him, and he shall make his appearance." Detective Goode's number flashed on the screen. "He really wants to talk to you."

"Like I said, he can wait." I stroked Sunlight's furry head and rocked myself back and forth. "I've got much more important things to worry about."

Like my gorgeous cat, my time with Gamma and Lauren, Christmas coming up, and beyond that, the very bright and exciting future.

Finally, I had started taking steps to be the person that Gossip needed me to be. I would never look back, only forward to the shimmer on the horizon. A life with the cats, my grandmother, and a real purpose. I couldn't wait.

Charlie and Gamma's adventures conclude in the show-stopping finale of The Gossip Cozy Mystery series, The Case of the Diabolical Decadence.

CRAVING MORE COZY MYSTERY?

If you had fun with Charlie and Gamma, you'll want to meet Milly and her pet bunny Waffle. You can read the first chapter of Milly's story below!

"It's unheard of! A travesty." My grandmother, Cecelia Pepper, sat on the edge of her seat at the coffee bar in the Starlight Cafe. "Why, the sheriff ought to be ashamed of himself. How are we meant to walk down the streets in this town with this... threat in the backs of our minds? Looming! Like some giant Sword of Damocles over our heads." She tapped the newspaper, a copy of *The Star Lake Gazette*, she'd laid on the coffee bar the minute she'd sat down.

My grandmother was the definition of dynamite in a small package. At 75-years-old, she was brimming with vigor to make up for her height.

"I'm sure Sheriff Rogers will figure it out." I fixed Gran a cup of coffee—a hazelnut latte with extra cream—and placed it in front of her. "It's a small town, Gran. They'll catch whoever's doing this."

"A small town that's going downhill quickly." My grandmother glanced around as if she was afraid of someone overhearing our conversation.

But the painful truth was there was nobody in my cafe this morning. Just like there'd been nobody in it the day before.

As I'd learned quickly, folks in Star Lake, Iowa, were insular. They didn't care that my late father, a town favorite, had left me the cafe. I hadn't lived in town long enough for them to trust me, and then there was the fact that I had absolutely no experience in the hospitality industry.

Not now. Just take a breath and smile.

"I mean, really. A mugger? Here? Nancy from the bakery told me her sister's best friend's cousin was attacked. Wallet stolen. Can you believe that? If I didn't love the lake and the people so much," my grandmother continued, lifting the latte, "I'd move away in a heartbeat."

"Gran."

"I'm serious."

"Gran, you've lived here for thirty-five years."

"Fine. I might not move, but I'll protest this at the

next town council meeting. You can mark my words on that." Gran took a sip of her latte, pressed her lips together and fluttered her eyelashes. "Nearly as good as your father used to make."

A silence ensued, filled with our shared sorrow. It was too soon to talk about him.

I cast my gaze away from Gran and studied the interior of the cafe. Light streamed through the windows and the glass front doors, illuminating the linoleum that was in need of a revamp, as well as the checked tablecloths and laminated menus. The chairs were comfortable and well worn. The cash register was an antique and the walls were dark wood.

Overall, the aesthetic was typical of my dad's taste. Hastily thrown together but with plenty of heart.

"This really is good." Gran must've noticed the lump in my throat. Metaphorically, of course. "You know, you'll make a fine restaurant owner. As fine an owner as you would've made a detective."

That was another touchy subject. "Thanks, Gran." I forced a smile.

She reached over and patted my forearm.

Movement outside on the brick-paved sidewalk caught my attention. A homeless woman, wearing a shabby coat and carrying several plastic bags, walked up and took a seat outside the cafe.

"Oh dear," Gran said.

CRAVING MORE COZY MYSTERY?

"Do you know her?"

"Only by sight," Gran replied. "She's new to town I think. I'm not familiar with her story. Poor woman."

I bit down on my lip then headed back to the coffee machine and started fixing another latte. Much to my surprise, the bell over the door tinkled, and Sheriff Rogers entered.

He was in his late fifties, with a gray mustache, balding, and wearing his uniform with pride. He sauntered over to the bar and eyed me. "Morning."

"Good morning, Sheriff," I said. "What can I get for you today?"

The sheriff didn't immediately answer me. He scanned the interior of the cafe then pointed over to a new section I'd set up, with the help of my cook, Francesca. "What's that?"

"That's the waffle station," I said, smiling. "Do you want to try it out? We prepare the waffles fresh, bring 'em out to you, and then you decorate them as you see fit. There's ice cream and maple syrup, there's—"

"That wasn't here when Frank was running the place."

"No," I said. "No, it wasn't. I figured that people would enjoy—"

"Waffles?"

"Sheriff Rogers," my grandmother said, and the sheriff jumped a little.

"Celia." He sniffed, using Gran's nickname. "Shoot. I

didn't see you there." And he sounded truly regretful, like he was anticipating a volley of complaints. He wouldn't have been wrong in that respect.

"What's this I hear about a mugger?" Gran tapped the newspaper. "A mugger in our midst?"

"Well, yeah, there have been reports of muggings over the past week, but I assure you it's under control."

"Now, Sheriff, you know better than to shovel that level of manure around me," Gran said. "I want answers, and I want them now. What am I supposed to tell the ladies in my book club? That we can't walk to the library in peace?"

"I assure you..."

The conversation faded out as I finished off the latte, grabbed a cupcake from the display of about a dozen under the glass counter, and walked out into the sunlight.

It was the end of summer, the weather a temperate 70 degrees with a soft breeze brushing down the street. I stopped in front of the homeless woman.

"Good morning," I said.

She glared at me, her skin tan, and her ire obvious. "What do you want, Red?"

The urge to brush my fingers through my red hair nearly overtook me. Thankfully, my hands were full. "Uh."

"Let me guess. You want me to move. It's a free country, you know, I—"

"No," I said. "I just wanted to check if you were OK."

"OK?"

"Yeah." I handed her the coffee and the cupcake. "You need anything?" It was my experience, after working as a beat cop in the city, that everyone had a story. Just like everyone had a purpose. Sometimes life just... got in the way.

The woman blinked. "Uh. Yeah. I'm good. Thanks."

"Sure. Just holler if you need a glass of water or something," I said. "I'll be inside."

The woman, still full of mistrust, nodded then took a sip of her coffee. I headed back into the cafe and found Gran and Sheriff Rogers embroiled in their argument.

"—muggers on the streets. If you think that we'll stand for this then you're delusional. You know, I can call up the heads of the three factions, right now, and get them to arrange a meeting."

Sheriff Rogers, blustery as he was, paled at that.

The "factions" as they were called, were the three unions that pretty much ran Star Lake. There were "the boaters", "the butchers", and "the bakers"—and they frequently disagreed on issues, to the point where the town was practically split into three. It was expected that you'd fall into line with one of the groups even if you weren't an active member of said union.

"The bakers would be most interested to hear about your lack of action when it comes to crime on our

CRAVING MORE COZY MYSTERY?

streets. I mean, this whole area is packed with bakeries and restaurants. This is bound to affect tourism too. And then the boaters will get antsy."

The summer months in Star Lake were famed for their fun boating activities, from tours on the lake, to fishing, to jet skiing and recreational activities.

"You're complaining about mugging and crime on the street," Sheriff Rogers said, finding his voice, "yet you won't stop your granddaughter over here from feeding said criminals."

Gran jerked back as if she'd been slapped—a strange effect on a tiny woman in a floral-print dress. "Feeding them? I think the heat is getting to you, Sheriff."

"She just took out a coffee and a cupcake to..." He trailed off and gestured toward the homeless woman now sitting on a bench out front.

"And so?" Gran grew red and rose from her barstool, trying to tower at four feet eight inches.

The sheriff tugged on his collar. "All I'm saying is that if you don't want trouble, don't invite it into your home." And with that, he swept from the cafe, trailing his overbearing spicy cologne.

"Idiot," Gran muttered.

"Gran."

"There's no love lost between us." She resumed her seat. "And for good reason."

But she didn't go into the reason. I fixed a cup of

coffee for Francesca, who was in the kitchen, patiently awaiting orders that would likely never come, and then joined my grandmother at the counter.

Gran paged through the newspaper, stopping on an image and tapping it. "See, now, this is why you don't want to get on the wrong side of those boaters. Look at that. A full page ad for their 'Boating Blowout 2021.'"

I read over her shoulder. "Join us for a boating extravaganza as we celebrate the end of summer."

"You're going, I assume? Everyone's going," Gran said. "Everybody who's anybody. It will be a great opportunity for you to network, dear. It's been a year, and you've only made one friend."

"Thanks, Gran."

"I'm just saying," she replied, "that it might be a good opportunity for you to get out there and meet someone."

"Meet someone? The only person I'm interested in meeting is an accountant who can help me manage my finances for this place." Things were *not* looking good. And I was *not* about to let down my father's legacy by losing the Starlight Cafe.

"I'm sure there are plenty of eligible accountants around."

"Not what I meant, Gran."

She gave me a sneaky smile, and it cheered me up. I couldn't stay mad at Gran.

"Are you coming by tonight for supper?" Gran asked.

"I'm making chicken casserole. You can bring Waffle along."

"That sounds great."

It sure beat eating a microwave dinner over the kitchen sink.

Want to read more? You can grab **the first book on all major retailers.**

Happy reading, friend!

PAPERBACKS AVAILABLE BY ROSIE A. POINT

A Burger Bar Mystery series

The Fiesta Burger Murder

The Double Cheese Burger Murder

The Chicken Burger Murder

The Breakfast Burger Murder

The Salmon Burger Murder

The Cheesy Steak Burger Murder

A Bite-sized Bakery Cozy Mystery series

Murder by Chocolate

Marzipan and Murder

Creepy Cake Murder

Murder and Meringue Cake

Murder Under the Mistletoe

Murder Glazed Donuts

Choc Chip Murder

Macarons and Murder

Candy Cake Murder

Murder by Rainbow Cake

A Milly Pepper Mystery series

Maple Drizzle Murder

A Sunny Side Up Cozy Mystery series

Murder Over Easy

Muffin But Murder

Chicken Murder Soup

Murderoni and Cheese

Lemon Murder Pie

A Gossip Cozy Mystery series

The Case of the Waffling Warrants

The Case of the Key Lime Crimes

The Case of the Custard Conspiracy

The Case of the Butterscotch Burglar

The Case of the Shortcake Serenade

A Mission Inn-possible Cozy Mystery series

Vanilla Vendetta

Strawberry Sin

Cocoa Conviction

Mint Murder

Raspberry Revenge

Chocolate Chills

Made in the USA
Middletown, DE
17 June 2024

55954275R00078